SLOW [...]
IN P[...]

SLOW DEATH
IN PARIS

Denis Belloc

Translated by William Rodarmor

QUARTET BOOKS

First published in Great Britain by Quartet Books Limited 1992
A member of the Namara Group
27/29 Goodge Street
London W1P 1FD

Originally published in France as *Képas* in 1989
by Lieu Commun
Copyright © 1989 Lieu Commun
Translation copyright © 1991 by William Rodarmor

Translator's dedication:
For Thaisa Frank

British Library Cataloguing in Publication Data

Belloc, Denis, *1949*–
    Slow death in Paris.
    I. Title
    843.914 [F]

ISBN 0 7043 2787 2

Phototypeset by Intype, London
Printed and bound in Great Britain by
BPCC Hazells Ltd
Member of BPCC Ltd

To Jacques,
To Isabelle,
For silent cries.

I

Your nose runs and sniffles, your eyes, with their dilated pupils, stare vacantly through tears. Your cheeks are hollow and your pale, your shivering body is cut by a line of pain that starts in your kidneys, circles your waist, and stabs into your guts. Your legs feel heavy and tired, and you hawk and spit every twenty paces. It's a sickness.

You're forever making the same circuit: Maine–Vandamme–Gaîté–Edgar-Quinet streets, back and forth, again and again, always at night, when it's cold, but you're even colder inside, along your bones. If you have five francs, you sit at the Liberté and order a cup of coffee that you don't drink, just to be sitting down, to ease the pain. On the circuit or at the Liberté, you recognize each other by the sickness. You don't know each other's names, or, if you once did, you've forgotten them; your memory's sick too. Talk is fast and choppy, in hoarse, frightened voices: 'Seen Pockface anywhere?' 'No, that sod's a pain. When did you last turn on?' 'An hour ago.' 'And it's two, three o'clock in the morning. What a fucker that bloke is.' 'You're right. Fucking Pockface.'

Saadi the Tunisian used to sell the remedy for our

3

sickness, but there were so many addicts between Maine and Edgar-Quinet that he took on a street-seller, a Portuguese with a face full of pock-marks who's also a junkie.

The remedy comes in a little piece of paper folded in eight like a little parcel, but junkies don't call it a 'parcel', they call it a 'wrap-up' or a 'wrap'. Junkies have their own words for everything.

There's powder in the wrap. Light brown if it's Pakistani ('Paki'), or dark brown, white, yellowish-white, pink. Whatever the colour, it's 'smack', 'junk', 'shit', 'horse', or 'H'. Heroin. Junkies snort the remedy up their noses, using a tube of rolled-up paper or tin-foil; or they 'shoot up' ('get a hit' or a 'fix'), sticking the needle of a syringe (a 'spike', or 'hypo') in a vein in their arm, hand, or foot, in the jugular, in the eye, under the tongue, in the penis.

Smack is expensive, two hundred francs for a wrap, four hundred for half a gram, eight hundred for a gram (a 'G'). White heroin costs more, a thousand or twelve hundred francs a gram.

You pour the smack into a spoon, add a few drops of lemon juice or vinegar to dissolve the powder, add some water, then heat it just until the mixture starts to quiver. Then you drop a filter into the spoon – a bit of cotton-wool or a cigarette filter – draw the liquid up into the syringe, tie off your arm with a belt, tap your skin to bring up the vein, and shoot. You draw up a bit of blood and push the plunger. You might repeat the process a few times, 'flushing'. It doesn't do anything, it's just a habit, a way of ending the ceremony. White heroin doesn't require heating or lemon juice:

4

just water and a filter, that's all. Junkies keep their filters; on days without dope, they give good juice.

Smack is never pure; it's cut with milk sugar, strychnine, rat poison, arsenic, crushed aspirin or other drugs.

Smack 'hits', 'rushes', 'flashes', or 'comes on'.

'Scoring' or 'copping' means buying smack.

When you've had a hit, you're 'loaded', 'turned on', 'ripped', 'cool', 'stoned', or 'on the nod'. When you can't score, you're 'hurting', 'itchy', or 'in hell'. When they're hurting but can't cop smack, junkies buy codeine-based cough medicines like Nétux or Néo-codion,[†] and swallow twenty, forty, or even sixty doses. At sixty, you throw up.

Some junkies say they're just 'joy-popping', that they're not hooked; they're 'clean', not dossers. Junkies are followed by the cops. Sometimes they get tired of the remedy, tired of being hooked, and they kick the habit, 'get clean' or 'get well'. And sometimes they wind up with too much smack in their syringes, and die of an overdose: 'OD'. Sometimes it's an accident; more often, they've just packed it in.

[†] Similar to Benylin in the UK, or Romilar in the US. (*Translator's note*)

I've been waiting for hours and there's no sign of Pock-face. I don't have five francs to buy coffee at the Liberté, just enough money to buy my wrap, so I'm resting my wasted body against the grillwork at the Edgar-Quinet métro station. Over by the cemetery, a crowded group of shadows stands motionless, the light catching their worn trainers and tattered jackets. I'll have to chase Pockface down to get served quickly, otherwise those dossers will score all the wraps. Across the intersection, a girl is waiting under the neon lights of a launderette. I've seen that face somewhere before, with its dark eyes and black hair, cheeks still full. I drag my body across to the neon lights, ask the girl if she's waiting for Pockface. She says she is, but hasn't seen the bastard, or Saadi, for that matter, or even Ciel, Pockface's girl-friend, a tiny Portuguese woman who shoots three Gs a day into her jugular.

'What about the blokes over by the cemetery, you know them?' 'They aren't from around here. You see how they look? Junkies, dossers. Jesus, they're a mess . . .'

We head up rue de la Gaîté. When we talk, we start every sentence with the same words: Christ, fuck, shit.

6

The sickness has eaten up our vocabulary. Can we shoot up together? the girl wants to know; it isn't as strange when there are two of you, and shit, she's completely wrecked tonight. Everything the bint's wearing is black: a mangy fake-fur coat, trousers, rubber beach-sandals, her plastic carrier. Even the spaces between the stumps of her teeth are black. She walks on her toes, looks as if she's dancing. She wants to give me her dosh – I don't know you, but I trust you – that way, when Pockface shows, I can jump on him and score for both of us before the down-and-outs crowd around.

Pockface shows up at the corner of Gaîté and Vandamme, my heart's pounding in my chest, he's walking fast without stopping, his riddled face held high, pupils blown wide open. He always carries a book or a newspaper or magazine. You first have to slip your dosh between the pages, then he'll serve you the smack.

'Hi, there. What the fuck's been keeping you?'

'If you don't like it, go and score somewhere else.'

'Don't get uptight. I'm hurting, it makes me speedy.'

'What do you want?'

'Three wraps. Why don't you ever have any halves?'

'I'm not the one who makes up the wraps, it's Saadi. Anyway, two wraps are the same as a half.'

'You know damned well it isn't the same. There's always more than two wraps in a half!'

'Like I said, if you don't like it, you can go and score somewhere else.'

I shut up. If Pockface gets angry he won't want to serve me. Shaking, I lay the money between the pages of his open book.

'That took forever!' the girl says. 'I thought you'd got hung up.' She doesn't have her works and all the chemist's shops are closed. I have a syringe that's only been used once, I tell her, and my place isn't far; just on the other side of Montparnasse station. Am I HIV-positive? she wants to know. I have no idea, but I lie: 'No, don't worry. Besides, I never shoot up after anyone else.' She's only too happy to use a syringe that's just been used once.

We aren't walking now, we're running, but the pain in our guts has started to change, to become more bearable. I finger the wraps in my pocket, trying to guess how full they are. One of them doesn't feel as thick, so I give it to the girl in black.

I take a lemon from my fridge, the syringe and some cotton-wool from a fake wood salad-bowl. I fill two glasses with water, one to shoot with, the other to rinse out the spike. My strap is a red elastic belt with a metal buckle, flecked with blood. I tie off the girl in black's arm. She just has one hole in her vein.

'I always shoot at the same place so as not to have needle tracks,' she says. She jabs the needle in, pulls on the plunger; no blood appears in the syringe. Sweating, she starts probing around in her arm. 'Shit, I'm going mad. Tighten it some more.'

I tighten the belt. The syringe turns red. The girl in black's pupils shrink, her eyes start to glisten.

In turn, she tightens the belt around my forearm.

'You shouldn't shoot up in your wrist.'

'Higher up, there's nothing doing; I've used the vein too much, it has to heal. Anyway, I don't care about having tracks.'

I find the vein on the first try, shoot the smack home. I flush three times.

Pockface's Paki comes on great. It warms your body,

makes you forget about your guts, your legs, and the war inside your skull. It eats away pain – all sorts of pain. In my diary, I write 'ı WS' for 'one wrap shot' in the evening section. 'ı WS' appears in each of the morning sections, 'ı WS' each evening. The girl in black is smoking a Camel, sitting on a metal chair as colourless as her vacant eyes, looking at my single room, the kitchen in the corner, the wooden steps leading to the loft, to the bathroom with the chemical toilet, to the bed. She tells me her name's Ida. Her head's bent, her chin sunk on her chest. An easel stands at the back of the room; unframed paintings are stacked along the walls. A shelf runs under the windows, loaded with brushes, tubes of paint, charcoals – all covered with dust. The ash from the Camel falls to the grey, blood-stained carpet.

'You paint?' she asks.

'Used to. But I don't feel like it anymore.'

An Olympia typewriter sits on the white plywood table.

'You write detective stories?'

'Not really.'

I tell her about the story I wrote, about a kid with a big emptiness inside. A kid in pain.

'And it hurts him?'

'Read it for yourself.'

I give her a copy of the kid-in-pain story. She wants a dedication, so I write, 'For Ida. Powder and blood.' She says she's really pleased, that if she knew how to do all that, paint and write, she wouldn't do smack. After a moment's thought, she says she doesn't understand why I do.

'Has it been a long time?'

9

'I don't remember anymore . . . Maybe a year.'

That wakes her up.

'Christ, is that all? Me, it's been five . . .'

'How old are you?'

'Twenty. I'll be twenty this summer. You think I look older?'

'No, no, you don't look older.'

'I've got to get my teeth fixed. They make me look older.'

She says she's completely wrecked: 'Jesus, why do you do it, anyway?' Ida's a pain, wanting to know everything, so I tell her how I first got hooked on smack.

★ ★ ★

It's a cold January evening near Montparnasse station. The man's ahead of me on the escalator, wearing a grey hat and a dark blue overcoat. He turns round and looks at me. He walks out of the station, I follow, he enters the Hotel Méridien car park. On the second level down, he opens his coat and drops his trousers to his ankles. I unbutton my jeans, we feel each other's cocks. He asks me if I want to take him, I say yes, I stick my cock up the man with the grey hat's arse. I come very quickly. We say goodbye.

An April evening in the station. The man's wearing his dark blue coat, but not the grey hat. Pepper-and-salt hair rings his bald scalp. He's waiting near the lavatories, over by 'Grandes Lignes'. In the car park, he asks me if I feel like taking it, but I say, 'Not tonight.' I don't like men to fuck or kiss me. The man bends over. We leave the garage together.

'Where are you heading?'

10

'This way.'

'Me too.'

We talk about how cold it was this winter, hope the weather's good this summer. As we chat about this and that, he asks me if I know the time difference between Paris and Tokyo.

'I don't know. Probably seven or eight hours.'

He has to make a call to Japan. When we get to my street, we say goodnight.

It's late summer, the weather's fine. The man's in front of the station, wearing a blue jacket and trousers. He wants to go somewhere else, I suggest my place.

He strips under the wooden ladder that leads up to the bed with its navy-blue quilt, takes off his gold-rimmed glasses. His eyes are round and sad, his mouth small, his lips thin and curved. His body is heavy and powerful, and large moles dot his back. We fuck on the navy-blue quilt without speaking. He wants me to take him, but just then I lose my hard-on. He says, 'I'll get you hard again, you'll see,' and kisses me. I let him do it, and my cock stiffens. When I come this time, it feels different. My orgasm is stronger and lasts longer, as I concentrate on this bloke between my legs.

While he's pulling on his clothes, he looks at the canvas on the easel, but doesn't say anything. I write my phone number on a piece of paper and tell him my name. He gives me his number – he runs a school for handicapped children – tells me his name is Jerome. The blue jacket zips shut. He shakes my hand and says goodnight as casually as if he were asking a greengrocer for a pound of spuds.

His face and body stick in my mind. I make love to the

images several times, and as the hours of the night stretch out, the images blur and disappear. I smoke a lot of fags and have trouble getting to sleep. I'm thinking he should never have kissed me.

Jerome says these meetings at the station must be coincidences, but they aren't: I've been lying in wait for him. On Sunday evenings, too. He's waiting over on the 'Grandes Lignes' side with a suitcase in his hand, says he's just back from the country, where he has a house on a big sloping plot at the edge of a wood.

It's the end of the summer holidays, his school has gone back, I find his telephone number. 'Can we get together?' 'If you like.' Jerome never says no. We see each other twice a week and on Sunday evenings.

The canvas on the easel is finished: a woman's body, curled up, head bent, hair falling over her face. The woman's dress is pushed up on her thighs, her knickers and stockings are tangled around her ankles. Her knees are touching, her left shoe is missing. She's been raped. Jerome looks at the raped woman but doesn't say anything. He doesn't care. Since he doesn't care, it'll be my last painting.

On the first page of a notebook, I write sentences for Jerome, things I never say aloud. I find rhymes for the words, reread the page. Poems are stupid. I rip up the page.

On the second page, I write more words, ones that don't rhyme. I write a story, the story of a kid with a big emptiness inside. A kid in pain. I'm writing for myself. I'll dedicate the story to Jerome, though he'll

12

never read it. I write with hate at my fingertips, tapping at the Olympia:

She didn't want a boy, she wanted a girl, even had a name all picked out: Laura. And she spat me out between her legs. A girl or a boy, the father didn't give a damn, he was so wasted he probably didn't see what was hanging between my legs.

★   ★   ★

'Let's get out of here, Ida. When I've shot up, I can't stand hanging around my place.'

It's freezing outside, but we feel warm. Along Gaîté, an old junkie asks after Pockface, we say we don't know, we've already scored. The bloke's hurting, but we don't give a damn. We feel good.

'Try over on Réaumur!'

'It's all crap on Réaumur. Those fucking blacks always rip you off!'

'Sorry, man, can't do a thing for you.'

The old chap goes shakily towards the métro. Ida has twenty francs left; she buys chips and two *merguez* sausages at a Tunisian hole in the wall. We dig into the greasy parcel and talk about constipation.

'In the morning, I eat breakfast first, then go to the bog, then I shoot up. If I shoot beforehand, I can't have a crap, dope makes me constipated.'

For her, everything's normal, she's regular. Anyway, she never shoots up in the morning.

'Only real junkies get loaded first thing in the morning,' she says. 'The ones who are wasted, really hooked.'

It's when she takes Néos that she can't go.

13

'What shit those Néos are.'

★ ★ ★

There's a shower on a hose in the bidet, you have to sit on the edge of the bidet to wash. I sit down, shoot the water up inside me, and go and squat on the toilet while holding the water in. Water and shit spurt out together. Bidet, toilet, I repeat the process a couple of times to loosen my sphincter, to make my insides clean so when Jerome's cock fucks me, it'll stay clean. Spotless. When the water finally squirts out clear, I grease my hole with lubricant: genuine Chesebrough-Pond's vaseline.

'Take me,' I tell Jerome, and the pleasure explodes in my arse, my body, my head. When he fucks me, he calls me 'darling', but he probably calls all the blokes he fucks or who fuck him 'darling'.

I pick Jerome's hairs from the navy-blue quilt. I know they're his: they're thick and straight, pepper-and-salt. Mine are finer, black and curly. I put the hairs in an envelope which I often open. I feel its contents with my fingertips, sniffing the hairs a long time.

I kiss Jerome's face, his nose, his cheeks, his forehead, his chin, his lips, right eye, left eye. I run my fingers over every part of his face. It gets on Jerome's nerves; this isn't an anatomy lesson, he says. All the same, he kisses my face the same way one day.

★ ★ ★

I'm seven years old, we're on the Invalides concourse, she's holding my hand, I'm not afraid any more. When I'm

14

away from her I feel like an abandoned child. We're out for a walk on a Thursday afternoon, my father's been dead for a long time. She's my whole universe.

★   ★   ★

It's a weekday evening, a Tuesday without children. I spread my legs, and when he's inside me, murmur, 'Oh, Jerome.' It just came out, he pretended not to hear. He pulls on his coat and suggests we get a bite to eat at a little restaurant he goes to from time to time.

He orders an *andouillette* with mustard sauce. When it comes, he says it's beautiful, 'A great-looking banger for a half-arsed arse-banger.' I don't get it. Halfway through his sausage, he starts to talk. Eyes lowered, he starts telling me about himself for the first time: the year was 1942, the man and the woman weren't married, the man got the woman pregnant and took off. An embryo was in the woman's belly, the family and people said she was going to be an unmarried mother, that it was shameful, it's with a husband that you make babies. The woman stood on a bridge over the Seine, she wanted to climb over the railing to drown herself and drown the thing inside her guts. The woman didn't jump, the embryo became a body. One day, it was the thing's baptism. At the church, the priest said he wouldn't have the bells rung, they're forbidden for unmarried mothers. Jerome isn't the one telling the story. It's the child inside her guts.

At the corner, we say goodnight. He stretches out his hand, I kiss him on the mouth. He's furious, and backs away, saying he hates doing that. Never in the street, he says.

★   ★   ★

15

I'm ten years old. She says he waited two years after the man died to ask her to marry him. She says she refused, it was too soon, she was still wearing black and she didn't like this man. One day she said yes, the man wanted a child, a girl. She was sure it was a girl and she spat a girl out from between her legs. She isn't my universe anymore.

★ ★ ★

We eat our chips and *merguez*, then order two coffees at the Liberté. I ask Ida if she's living with her mother. It's been an age since she lived with that bitch, she answers. The bitch was thirteen when someone first jumped her, but Ida isn't sure who her father is; there were a couple of blokes that day. The bitch wanted nothing to do with her daughter, so she stuck her with her mother. When she was ten, Ida went back to the bitch; there was a black bloke at the house. The black gave the bitch a kid, and one to another girl. He was living one day at the other girl's, one day with the bitch, who didn't give a damn: the black wasn't the only man in her life. Ida was fourteen when she saw something odd: the bitch's door was open, the black was on top of her and she was moaning. The black saw Ida and gave her an odd smile. Trembling, Ida went back to her room. The following year, she tried the remedy. It was going around at school, one of the blokes was even shooting up in class. One day he slipped Ida a line. At first nothing happened, but then the remedy started coming on, and Ida began to feel really cool. She was cool all evening, she even talked to the black and the bitch; normally, she didn't talk, she didn't dare, and besides, people bugged her. She started doing two or three lines a week, until one day the kid at

16

school said he couldn't turn her on for free anymore, that shooting up was where it's at. So she nicked a hundred francs from the bitch, and the bloke gave her her first shoot. She couldn't handle school anymore, wasn't keeping up. Too bad, she would have liked to go into social work, take care of kids, or something. At home, the bitch noticed Ida's dilated pupils, noticed that money was always missing from her purse. 'You've got to stop,' she told Ida. 'It's bad for your health.' She took Ida to a doctor who gave her medicine to help her kick the habit. This lasted a couple of weeks, and then she went back to the needle. The bitch started to cry. 'I can't take it anymore,' she said. 'One day I'll inject myself with you and we'll snuff it together!' Ida said she was fed up too, 'with you, with your black, and with school!' She grabbed a few clothes and took off. She found a job as a shop assistant where she was paid under the counter and stayed with mates and girlfriends, sometimes at her grandmother's. She liked the old lady, who was half Arab and half Jewish. From time to time she stole from the old lady's purse. She stayed with Nico, too, the bitch's brother, who had already had two ODs. She didn't call him 'Uncle'. They were the same age, so she called him 'ducks'. Ducks had everything you needed at his place, spikes and good Paki.

★ ★ ★

After he's done at the centre for handicapped kids, Jerome goes to a bar, the Bar de la Marine, and sits on the terrace. He sits motionless in front of a beer, his blue coat buttoned, hands flat on his knees. This isn't his first beer; there are several bills under his saucer.

17

Jerome's face is sad, his look vacant, and his eyes seem moist. One evening, I ask him if anything's wrong. Everything's fine, he answers with an ironic smile. I want to know what's eating him, so I ask again. His smile turns nasty, his eyes dry up, and he says that life is beautiful.

I stroll a while with him. Jerome's walk is heavy, his body jerks from side to side. He seems to be suffering, but the pain isn't in his body. It's somewhere else.

I go to the Marine every night and drink a lot of beer. White hairs, black hairs, the envelope is getting fatter. Jerome is eating away at me.

★   ★   ★

I'm twelve years old, I'm in a changing room at the Porte d'Orléans swimming pool. The man is old and very hairy, he's pulled down both of our swimming trunks. He wants me to suck his cock. I tell him I don't like that.

'Come on, just a little bit.'

I suck on his cock, but it turns my stomach.

'I can't!'

'OK, wank me off.' I masturbate the man.

'Stop! Stop!' But it's too late, he's coming. And he gives me hell. 'I told you not so fast, damn it, I didn't want to come. Now hop it!'

I step out of the changing room, it was very hot and humid in there. The stuff is running down my cheek, the man came on my face, as if to punish me.

I'm fifteen. My brother hands me a fifty-franc note. 'Take it, it's so you can go with a tart. Mum told me, "Give this to your brother, I never see him with girls, it must bother him. He's old enough now. But don't tell him the money came from me." So be careful, little bro', don't say I told you.'

There are whores in a little street near the Anvers métro station. I don't choose one, just ask the first woman I see how much she's asking.

'It's fifty, love, and twenty-five for the room. But hold on a minute, aren't you under-age?' I tell her I'm eighteen, she doesn't believe me.

'I really shouldn't . . . All right, come on.'

In the hotel hallway, an old woman hands the whore a towel.

'Give her a tip, ducks . . .'

I hand the old lady a couple of francs.

'What are you waiting for, love? Get undressed!'

We get undressed. I'm trembling.

'Come here and let me wash you.'

She washes me over the bidet.

'Give me your cash . . . You just have fifty francs? You aren't exactly loaded, are you, duckie? Lie down.'

I stretch out on the bed, the whore straddles my legs and sucks my cock. From time to time, she abandons my cock to toss her head, throwing back her oily black hair, which keeps falling across her face and keeps her from sucking properly. Each time she tosses her head, she sniffles.

'You really aren't in great shape, are you, love? Are you tired?'

I'm not tired, but this woman on my legs is my mother. She doesn't look like her, but I'm seeing her face, her body. My mother's the one sucking my cock, she's the one getting fed up, saying, 'Don't worry about it, duckie, these things happen. It'll be better next time.'

19

My brother asks how it went with the tart. 'Super,' I say.

'Did she get naked?'

'No, she kept her bra and a black thing on her stomach that held her stockings up. But I saw her hairs!'

'You just saw them, that's all? But you stuck your thing into her hairs, at least?'

'Hey, of course, what do you think?'

'Good, bro'. Mum will be pleased.'

I'm sixteen years old, my mother is cleaning a widower's flat. I'm in the bathroom, there's a pile of dirty laundry on the tiles: pants, a pair of socks, a T-shirt. Standing at the sink, I sniff the laundry and have a wank. A photo of a very beautiful woman is hanging on the bedroom wall. My mother says it was the widower's wife, that she hanged herself in the flat one day, and that ever since, the man's been living with the memory of her face hanging on the wall. One morning, I spit on the photo of the hanged woman.

★   ★   ★

'Have you ever been in love, Ida?'

She mulls this over. 'No, I don't think so.'

'Jesus, if you were ever in love, you'd remember! Why do you have to think about it?'

It comes to her. Yes, once, his name was Marc, she was pretty hung up on him, it lasted six or seven months. She can't remember why they broke up, it just happened. She was already shooting up at the time and he wasn't doing anything, that's probably what ended it.

'Anyway, sex isn't my thing.'

★   ★   ★

20

I'm seventeen, I'm in Toulon, sitting on a bench in a square next to a retired legionnaire who is stroking my thigh. It starts to rain, we leave the square, step into a doorway. I suck the legionnaire's cock and he slips me a hundred-franc note.

'No, that makes me feel weird. I don't do it for money.'

'Take it, it makes me happy. I live in Marseilles, you could come to my house, we'll do it in a bed and I'll give you a lot more.'

I take a train to Marseilles and we do it lying down. He talks about the Cameroon, the Rif war, Sidi-Brahim, Aurès-Nemenchas, Dien Bien Phu. And he gives me two hundred francs.

Back in Toulon, I learn that the widower has died and don't feel anything.

★ ★ ★

Jerome tells me another story in a Chinese restaurant, over spring rolls, Peking duck, and rosé de Provence. It was on a street in Pigalle, one evening a few years ago. He'd done a quickie with a chicken.[†] The cops nabbed Jerome, the chicken was under-age but Jerome couldn't tell, he seemed a lot older. Jerome stares at the bony carcass of his duck and talks about the shame. The night with the cops, the fear. He was suspended from his job with social security, and his friends and his trade-union turned their backs on him. He drinks a glass of rosé and says he put on a lot of weight during that time, had splitting headaches, and his blood pressure went up. He still takes a pill every morning to stop the pain in his head.

★ ★ ★

† Young male prostitute. (*Tr.*)

21

As far as money's concerned, Ida doesn't have too many problems. She makes six thousand francs a month under the counter as a shop assistant in a clothes shop in Créteil and spends it on smack. When she runs short, she borrows here and there, but she isn't complaining. She doesn't pay any rent, she's living with a bloke who puts her up: her husband. He's a Moroccan whom she married so he could get his papers and work in France, but she doesn't fuck him, he's too ugly. Sometimes, at night, he tries to feel her up, but Ida starts screaming and he lays off. The Moroccan doesn't work. He says he loves her.

They met in August. That month, she was sick of shooting her youth away. It was the month she turned nineteen and she wanted to get clean. Plane ticket for Casablanca, you have to get away to kick the habit, sunshine eats away the sickness. Five boxes of Néocodion in her suitcases, for the first days. In the terminal washroom, she gave herself a giant fix, her last one. She had never taken a plane before, didn't know if it was the altitude that did it, but the fix completely blew her mind: that evening, in Casablanca, she was still stoned! Eight days with a cousin of her grandmother's. Sunshine, the beach, couscous with Néocodion. Cool. Then a plane for Paris with her future husband, one of the cousin's mates. She lasted four months, carrying a fifth of whisky in her bag, which she drank straight from the bottle. A bottle a day.

'I wasn't talking to anyone, and I was getting aggressive. My face was all swollen, like an alkie's. I had to go back to smack.'

★ ★ ★

Jerome is in his white house on the hillside property, and I don't know what I'm doing on the sixth-floor landing of this building, drunk on beer and cheap red wine, standing in front of the door to the flat. I touch the door, listening, smelling Jerome. I leave, and am at the end of the hallway when the fucking door opens. The bloke has glasses and straight black hair.

'I wanted to see Jerome,' I stammer.

'He isn't here this weekend.'

'That's all right, I'll come back.'

The bloke is Japanese; he has the plug-ugly face of the Paris-Tokyo time difference. At the corner café, I knock back a couple of beers and some wine. Until I puke.

★   ★   ★

I'm eighteen, I'm at a get-together for queers in a queer bar: it's a 'girlfriend's' birthday. The man I live with – but don't love – is there. So are José, Bernard, Mariano, Robert, Saïd-Big-Dick, and Severino the handsome Yugoslav, in white jeans and white leather jacket, and the man who keeps him, a nicely turned out gent, coat-and-tie-lots-of-money-married-three-kids. His wife is mad about Severino, the man-I-live-with-but-don't-love tells me. Shouts and high-pitched laughter ring out, the girlfriend opens her presents: a pair of black lace knickers open at the back, a dildo, vaseline, sex toys.

'What's it like to go through the menopause, darling?

'Try the dildo, love, if it isn't the right size, I'll exchange it, but I'd be surprised if they come any bigger!'

'Happy birthday, ducks!'

The cake is shaped like a cock, dripping with custard. José feeds coins into the jukebox, the queers dance. Bernard

and Mariano are kissing. The man-I-don't-love has disap-
peared, as has Robert, so coat-and-tie-lots-of-money-mar-
ried-three-kids invites me to dance a slow number with him.
He lays his head on my shoulder, holds my waist tight.
He's sweating, I feel his lips on my neck, his sweat is
soaking me. I don't know how to dance, and I'm stepping
on his toes. On the last note of the soft music, he releases
my body and says, 'Thank you.' In a booth in the gay
bar, he caresses Severino and kisses him. The kiss lasts a
long time. They really look like they love each other. As
I'm watching them, I suddenly start to hurt; it's the first
time I've ever felt jealous.

Old Marcel comes in, shrieking, 'Well, it finally hap-
pened! My husband's dropped me . . . for a woman, too!
I mean, would you believe it, you bitches? It's too much!
Well, hello, don't mind me, girls! Feeling each other up
in front of a widow! Well, well! Happy birthday, you big
hunk!'

Old Marcel's never had a husband, I crease up laughing
and the pain subsides.

★　★　★

A beery night sends me up the walls, up to the skylight
roof, to spy on two sixth-floor windows in the building
across the way. In the right-hand one, behind the curtains, Jerome appears in the lamplight, he sits down in
a lighted area. My roof is one floor too low, so I can't
see the room's furniture, but it must be where they eat;
Jerome is gesturing like a man eating dinner. Then
Paris-Tokyo comes in and takes off his jacket. I can't
make out their faces but suppose they must be talking.
Jerome stands up, leaves the lit area, a light comes on
behind the slats of the left-hand window shutters; that

24

must be where they sleep. I come down from my sky-light. Light is shining through it from below. People were living under my feet.

I walk up to the sixth floor of the building across the way, glue my ear to the door, but can't hear anything. I climb on to one of the stools at the Bar de la Marine and order a beer. I drink a couple, then leave.

I climb the wooden steps up to the loft, collapse on to the navy-blue quilt, and bawl.

★ ★ ★

I'm nineteen, I'm on the boulevard de la Chapelle, a man is lying on the pavement, his hands and body twitching occasionally. His eyes are white, the pupils have disappeared, a pool of blood is spreading under his head. A crowd has gathered around the body. 'He's having a fit!' a woman shouts. Another one says we have to call an ambulance.

Nobody moves. The man looks dead, except that his body is alive. I look at the white eyes, the pool of blood under the living corpse's head, and I don't give a damn. I've arranged to meet a bloke by the Barbès métro, we'll go to a hotel on boulevard Rochechouart, we'll fuck and the bloke will give me money. I push my way out of the crowd, walk toward the bloke who pays to fuck. Barbès. I wonder if the body has stopped twitching.

★ ★ ★

'Twenty, thirty Ricards,' says Jerome. In the Pigalle joints, he drinks until he passes out, lying on a bench. A night of drinking *pastis*.

Making their rounds, the cops pick him up; Jerome has fallen off the bench. It's an emergency: Lariboisière hospital. Jerome comes to on the metal trolley and runs away. Twice before, he had drunk to the point of passing out, but he doesn't say why. Or for whom.

★ ★ ★

I'm twenty, I'm in bed with a man who calls me his sweetheart, his lamb, his love, his dream-boat. He says he loves me, that if I ever leave him, he'll commit suicide. He runs his hand along my arse, sticks his fingers in, asks me if I love him. I say that what he's doing is getting on my nerves, so he hisses between his teeth that I'm cold-hearted, incredibly cold, that I don't love anyone. I confirm it. 'You're right,' I say. 'I don't love anyone and pull your finger out, I don't want to be fucked any more.'

One day I leave the man and he doesn't commit suicide. I'm twenty, I'm still a kid. A dream-boat-in-pain.

★ ★ ★

It's late, the Liberté is emptying, there aren't any more addicts about on the Maine–Vandamme–Gaîté–Edgar-Quinet circuit. With Ida on my arm, I'm walking along Montparnasse.

'You seeing anyone, these days?'

'I've got something going with my boss but he's married.'

'So you go to hotels to fuck?'

'He hates hotels. We do it in the store-room . . . or in his delivery van.'

'Does he love you?'

'Oh, he says, "I love you, Ida", when he feels like fucking. Are you joking? It always happens at the end of the month, I get the feeling he screws me when his wife's having her period. For me, that's no problem: I

26

don't get my period anymore. Smack does that to you. Can't say that I miss it, mind, because when I was a kid, God, did it hurt. From time to time, I get a little something, just like that, without any warning, but it's nothing, see, just a few drops, it isn't even worth putting in a tampon. No, in that department, I'm laughing.'

★   ★   ★

Jerome's on holiday in the white house with his mother and his stepfather for the Christmas-tree-tinsel-lights-streamers-and-paper-hats holiday. When he comes back, we wish each other happy new year; I give him a gold ballpoint pen, and he gives me a fat book on the Impressionists: *Painters of Happiness*. It's Wednesday, a quiet day, a day without children. We drink a lot of red and white wine at the restaurant, we're kissing passionately in the headmaster's office. My trousers are around my ankles and Jerome is kneeling, sucking me. He wants me to come in his mouth. 'Give it all to me,' he says. (On the blue quilt, I want him to come in my mouth, but he always pushes my head away, saying he mustn't, that it isn't safe. I can come in his mouth, no problem: since the first time with him, at my place, I haven't touched any cock but his.) Jerome stands up, says we have to stop, that I have to leave.

'Go away!' His voice is pleading, and pain shows on his face. I don't understand anything anymore. I still haven't given Jerome what he wanted, and now I want him, in his office that smells of chalk. Crying, I pull up my trousers and swear at him. He's buttoned his trousers and is crying silently. I kiss him; it tastes salty. 'I love you,' I tell him. I love him like mad, like I never

27

have before, and that's something I've never said to anyone. He moves away from me and says we mustn't, we've got to forget about this, that he's not right for me. That's something I didn't understand when I was on my belly, legs spread, my arse offered, willing. For free. I ask him if we can get it together, anyway. He thinks for a moment, then says, 'Yes. Let's call each other tomorrow.'

★ ★ ★

The last page: after the man who didn't commit suicide, Dream-boat decides he doesn't want to be buggered anymore. He tells himself that one day, perhaps, he'll fall head over heels in love, really in love, and then – and only then – he'll offer his arse.

My friends seem to think that the kid-in-pain's arse is good enough to be published, so I Xerox it, put the copies in envelopes and post them. Destination: publishers.

I give the story to Jerome in his office. The next day, he says he saw colours in the typed pages. He says a few words about it. A single sentence.

★ ★ ★

March, a morning without children, in the Montparnasse tower complex. I'm following Jerome through the shopping centre. Unaware that I'm behind him, he looks in a shop window, takes the escalator. I know where he's going. He steps into the lavatories where men go to do more than piss: they look at each other above the urinals, touch each other, go into the stalls to fuck. Jerome's been in the lavatories for quite a while, too long for just a piss. I enter, hand the lavatory

28

attendant a franc. Jerome's standing alone at a urinal, waiting for the men who don't come there to piss. He comes out, says he looks like a fool, as usual. I don't know anything about the other times, he never told me. I'm smiling. He says it's finished, we aren't going to fuck anymore.

'It's better this way,' he says. My smile crumbles. His face is both hard and sad. 'I don't want to anymore.'

I climb on to the roof with the skylights, stick my ear against the sixth-floor door, open the envelope to smell his hairs, lie in wait for him at the Bar de la Marine, drinking one beer after another, station myself at the corner of the street and wait. Just to see him, touch his hand, say hello. We speak on the phone every day, eat out once a week.

In my diary, I write 'JT' for 'Jerome telephoned,' or 'TJ' for 'I telephoned Jerome.' Something is pounding under my ribs. It almost hurts.

I follow the man out of Montparnasse station. In the Méridien Hotel lavatories, I want him to fuck me. Until I'm sick of it. I haven't cleaned my sphincter, haven't greased myself, I pull down my jeans, turn around, grip the white porcelain of the urinal. I bend over, the man sticks his cock in. Something tears. A vision of Jerome's body before me, I clench my jaw. In silence, the man comes. He puts his tool away and says, ''Bye.' I hardly saw his face. Without bothering to squirt his come out of my guts, I return to the station. The geezer's old and toothless; in the station car park, I suck his limp cock. I unbutton his trousers to free his balls; the old geezer is wearing a leather hernia truss beneath his pants. I grab the leather, my mouth makes the limp cock stiffen, I drop my jeans and my pants, guide Old Toothless's cock to my arse. He loses his hard-on, I suck him off again, he comes in my mouth. I feel like puking. Stretched out on the navy-blue quilt, I haven't washed my arse, haven't emptied my guts, haven't rinsed my mouth. I'm crying. I have a wank, thinking of Jerome.

★　★　★

'Good morning madame, good morning sit down well it's none too warm I don't think we'll have much of a spring cut the cards with your left hand please are you a skin-diver oh no not me that's odd I see skin-diving yes that is odd give me thirteen cards with your left hand thank you no be careful not to cross your fingers it makes it hard for me to feel your vibrations well it isn't the best hand I've ever seen, still I see a big success in the artistic realm but not now later you'll have to be patient hand me some more cards aha but I do see a stable relationship yes stable and permanent I see two pairs of legs walking in the same direction is she younger than you? No he's older it's a man I don't like women, yes I suspected that I could tell from the hand you were dealt what a pity you're so handsome but I'm just saying that people are free to do as they please you know I don't have anything against homosexuals in fact I have many homosexuals among my customers, oh really? Yes and they're quite charming cut and give me thirteen cards yes but that relationship won't happen right away could this man have a bad character? . . . He has suffered a lot be very careful not to rush him or else he'll get his back up and it will be all over yes

30

do you feel you love him more than he loves you? Yes,
no that's not true but he is very shy and is afraid of
suffering more yes he is extremely sensitive what is
your sign? Libra with Leo rising, and him? Aries with
Virgo rising, my my Aries and Virgo that's not a good
mix Aries men are headstrong and passionate and
Virgos are full of calculated reserve and analyse their
feelings too much and hold Aries back when you met
were you in a crowd? Oh yes, I see, at a cottage, oh
no in the place we met there wasn't any cottage, oh
really that's curious I'm getting a cottage in any case be
patient and don't rush him so there it is that will be
four hundred francs I prefer cash if you don't mind,
not at all here you go thank you and don't worry
everything will work out goodbye goodbye and thank
you.'

★   ★   ★

It's night, we're on a bench on boulevard Sébastopol.
We got pretty pissed at the restaurant and had a row.
Leaving the restaurant, Jerome steps into a wine-bar
and drinks a cognac, then a second in another bar. He
spots me following him. 'What are you tailing me for?'
Jerome asks. 'Clear off! Leave me alone.' I tell him I'll
follow him to the end, until he collapses in the gutter,
and then I'll bring him home to his place. Jerome's
pissed, he wants to drink until he passes out. We sit
down on a bench. I'm crying, asking Jerome why he
strung me along all those months while he was fucking
me.

'Why did you do that?'

'That's not true! I wasn't playing with you. Maybe
it was a game in the beginning, but not afterwards.'

'What was it, then?'

Jerome doesn't answer, he never answers.

'You mustn't ever do that again!' I scream. 'You understand? To anyone!'

Jerome shrugs, gets up, walks into a wine-bar, orders a cognac. I wait outside on the pavement. Staggering, he brushes along a wall that's grey with night. I'm walking behind him, he turns around, tells me to go away, to leave him in peace. I grab him by the collar of his blue coat and tell him he's coming home with me. He slides down the wall and collapses on to the pavement. He wants me to leave him there, lying on the pavement. I pull him to his feet and tell him that I can't bear to see him in this state, that he doesn't deserve it, that I love him.

'Christ! I love you! You're being a pain in the arse! I'm calling a taxi and taking you home!'

Jerome gives me a nasty smile. His voice is nasty too, but calm.

'You want to hit me, is that it? Go ahead, hit me, you're dying to!'

'I've never hit anybody!'

'Are you sure?'

No, I'm not. I had once slammed my fist into the face of the man who didn't commit suicide. Jerome read about it in the kid-in-pain's story. But I don't want to hit him, I want to kiss him. Still holding Jerome by the collar, I prop him up against a parked car and hail a cab. In the taxi, I stroke Jerome's hand; he snatches it away. Smiling, I stroke his neck; he pushes my hand off. I lay it on his thigh and he leaves it there until the end of the ride.

I help Jerome into the lift. On the sixth floor, I wait

on the landing until he enters his flat. I can hear Paris-
Tokyo talking. 'Go to sleepy-bye,' says Jerome sweetly.
The other one keeps nattering. 'Go to sleep and stop
bugging me!' Jerome screams. The door closes. Out on
the landing, listening, I hear the toilet flush, Jerome's
vomiting. Between two heaves, he says, very loudly,
'Bastard, bastard, bastard!' The bastard tiptoes away.

On the telephone with Jerome:
  'But why me? What makes me so special?' he asks.
  'I have no idea, that's just the way it is. You can't
explain feelings like that. It just hits you all at once,
like a punch in the face. Can you explain that?'
  Jerome shuts up. He can't explain anything.

★ ★ ★

'Where did you used to score?' asks Ida.
  'Saint-Germain, rue de Buci, Saint-Michel. I took
my first snort in Saint-Germain. Most of my friends
who were hustling in Saint-Germain were doing
smack.'
  'You hustled in Saint-Germain?'
  'Not for long. A couple of months. Out of disgust,
or something. When Jerome dropped me, I completely
cracked up. I'd tell myself, you're nothing but a shit,
you're no better than the hustlers that Jerome buys. It
was a comeback: I used to hustle in Pigalle when I was
a kid.'
  'I've never hustled for smack, I couldn't.'
  'But it wasn't for smack, in the beginning, anyway.
I was disgusted with myself, like I said.'
  'Shit! I'm going to miss the last métro.'
  We swap phone numbers.

'Call me tomorrow at the shop. If you like, we'll go and score together tomorrow night.'

We kiss.

''Bye, Ida.'

I don't feel like going home. I climb the stairs to the plaza in front of the Montparnasse tower and lean on the railing. The rue de Rennes is in front of me, and, right at the end of the street, the pavements of Saint-Germain-des-Prés.

II

Fred the Tunisian is there, a veteran of fifteen years of hustling. He'll be forty soon, but doesn't look it except close up ('You see the bags under his eyes?' 'I'm sure he dyes his hair!'). Fred's got a phoney smile, a big car, and, according to the hustlers who've turned tricks with him, a lot of money ('Christ, the gear he's got: telly, hi-fi, VCR, and those shoes: three pairs of Westons!'). Fred gets busted every week for hooking: the copper always nails him in front of the other hustlers, but Fred just shouts at him and tears up the ticket. The hustlers all scatter when the filth stage a raid, but Old Fred never budges. Fred isn't much liked; they say there's something fishy about him, that he's an informer. Fred hangs out with Christian, who's been hustling for ten years. Christian wears his hair very long, trimmed to a point between his shoulder blades. He's always speedy, sometimes he says hello, sometimes not, his nose white with cocaine that he hasn't snorted properly.

Then there's Big Michel: blue eyes, a strong mouth, long, thin body. Michel's twenty-three, with two years on the street. And there's Dimitri, with his colourless eyes, who staggers along in oversized jeans and a dirty jacket, his bare feet stuck in what might once have been

37

a pair of trainers. Pierre, Big Michel's mate, shows up early, at about six o'clock, with a plastic carrier in his hand: in the carrier he's got a wallet, a book, a pen, and some clothes he's nicked from a shop. At ten, he takes the métro to go hustling over by Porte Dauphine. Martine and Jean are there early, too, each carrying a little backpack. It's harder for her: Saint-Germain isn't for women. Some evenings, Jean gives Martine hell: 'Shit, what a pain in the arse you are! He was a punter, I tell you. You should have insisted!' When they make money in Saint-Germain or Dauphine, they sleep at a hotel; otherwise they sleep in cellars and shower at Montparnasse station. Martine's twenty, Jean's twenty-five; they're in love. And there's Sad the Tunisian, a handsome bloke who lives with a black punter. The punter has hustlers and Sad hustles punters, but that isn't his job. Sad's job is to hang around Saint-Germain and hit up the hustlers for money: 'Hey, have you got a hundred francs to lend me? I'll pay you back tonight, I've got a great set-up with a punter who splashes it around.' He also fences stolen goods: cameras, VCRs, credit cards. And then there's the Duchess, a tall snobbish queen who won't talk to anyone, always wears great clothes in the style of Saint-Germain in the mid-seventies. She eats ice cream on the Drugstore café terrace – and ice cream on the Drugstore café terrace costs an arm and a leg – and hustles with her arms folded on her chest, her chin in the air, looking as if she thinks her shit doesn't stink. 'A real poofter,' say the hustlers who don't like queers, who've all got women and hate the punters. Then there are the part-timers, and the ones who hustle elsewhere: the Trocadéro, Porte Dauphine, rue Sainte-Anne. The hustlers in the Trocadéro are older, more 'masculine', as they say, and it isn't smart to muscle in on their patch, there aren't enough customers to go around as it is. Porte Dauphine is the Black Hole, you have to suck off punters in their cars for a hundred francs, or even fifty, and sometimes fuck their women while they wank off. Rue Sainte-Anne is sheer hell. The further up the street you get, the more the hustlers are into smack, and they're all HIV-positive, and the old junkie-HIV-positive-Sainte-Anne hustlers don't like punks coming in from the outside. There's the kid, Jeannine. She's fifteen, shy and fat, always dressed like a little girl. Her grandmother has two dogs, a pair of disgusting mongrels, and Jeannine spends hours walking them every evening. One night it's the white one, the next the black one. Jeannine smokes Marlboros, she knows all the Saint-Germain hustlers, and they're always hitting her up for smokes. There's fat Odila, the cop, who's got an enormous arse and a nose like a beacon; twenty-five years on the streets. And Facho, his partner, brown leather jacket, blond hair, steel-blue eyes. Odila will sometimes drag a hustler into a doorway to search him, and sometimes he feels the hustler's balls a little longer than necessary. Wouldn't surprise anyone if that big pile of shit were queer . . .

'You can stay around,' says Fred. 'No one'll muck you around. After all, everybody has to make a wack.'

When I was a punk in Pigalle, I used to lean against a tree or a wall and stay there; the punters would make the first move. Now you can't stand around, you've got to move, because of the cops. Now it isn't the punters who come on, it's the hustler. 'Good evening.

Looking for a boy?' Or, 'Looking for company?' I used to ask fifty francs; now, it's three hundred.

I'm pissed as I start street-walking: rue de Rennes, the Drugstore, a few steps down boulevard Saint-Germain. The man is short and blond. 'Good evening. Looking for a boy?' He's a Dane, he tried to withdraw money from a cash machine, but his card's expired, he's only got a hundred francs.

'What can I get for a hundred?'

'Not much. There's a car park in front of the Drug-store. I'll suck you off in there, if you like.'

That's fine with him. It's the first time he's ever paid to do it, he says. That's what punters always say, that it's the first time. I suck the Dane in the car park, he wants to touch my cock. 'No way. Not for just a hundred francs.'

He comes, and I spit it out. He says he wants us to get together again, at his place.

'Do you take cheques?'

'Why not?'

My first customer. I haven't lost my touch, but when the Dane came in my mouth I thought of Jerome, and nearly started crying.

* * *

Out on the hustlers' pavement, Christian is ranting. Saint-Germain is finished, he says; when he was starting out he'd turn two tricks at noon and two in the evening, and had plenty of money, but now, what with AIDS and smack, the customers don't want to fuck anymore. Fred says he feels like coming and asks Big Michel to wank him off. But Michel tells him to go fuck himself,

40

calls him an arsehole, says he's going to take on that fucker someday and put his fist up his nose. Big Michel just arrived, his blue eyes look strange. I ask him if he's been drinking.

'I don't drink. I do dope.'

'What kind of dope?'

'Smack.'

'What does smack do to you? Make you see things?'

'It's not that you see things, but when you've had a hit, you're cool, you don't think about anything, no more worries. You see the punters through rose-tinted glasses.'

He says all the hustlers here do smack except Fred and Christian. Martine and Jean share their dope, Dimitri shoots himself up in the foot. He can't shoot anywhere else, he doesn't have any veins left, that's why he doesn't wear socks. Dimitri's wrecked, dragging from morning till night, the punters don't want him anymore, so he begs and lets punters suck him off, or else he sucks for fifty francs, here and at Porte Dauphine. Big Michel isn't hooked, he can quit for a week without any problem by taking medicine that replaces dope. He buys his smack from Stéphane the Algerian, who deals between Saint-Michel and Montparnasse by way of Buci and Saint-Germain.

Sophie, Big Michel's woman, shows up. She hustles on the Champs-Elysées in the afternoon, turns a trick for five, six, or seven hundred francs, that's all she needs to buy her junk from Stéphane. Her eyes and hair are very black, she's tall and skinny, with a mouthful of rotten stumps. Big Michel is teasing her:

'When you aren't able to shoot up between your veins, you can shoot up between your teeth!'

41

'Lay off, goddamit! Don't you have anything better to do than give me grief over that? If you hadn't met that American punter who bought you a set of false teeth, you'd be worse than me.'

'So all you need is to find a punter who'll pay you for a set of teeth, you stupid cunt!'

I took the punter to my place. He wanted to fuck me on the navy-blue quilt but I didn't have any condoms and neither did he. I said, 'That's OK, go ahead the way you are,' but he said he didn't want to, because of AIDS. Then he wanted to kiss me, and I refused. 'Why don't you have a hard-on?' he asked. 'I'm taking anti-biotics,' I said. 'They do for you.' I wanted him to clear off fast, so I cut it short by sucking him off like a beast. He gave me the three hundred, his name – Alain – and his phone number at a posh bank job. As he was leaving, he said, 'Will I see you again sometime?' I answered, 'Whenever you like.' I rinsed my mouth out with Listerine, guzzled a litre of red wine straight from the bottle, and climbed on to the skylight roof. I could see Jerome; he was eating dinner. Then Paris-Tokyo showed up. I started crying like a fool on to the skylight roof, on to the people living under my feet.

At Saint-Germain an Arab stopped me, asked me if I wanted some stuff. I thought by 'stuff' he meant stolen goods, like VCRs and cameras.

'What kind of stuff?'

'Whatever you want: grass, hash, coke, H. I've got some terrific brown.' I nearly said yes, but instead said, 'No, I've got everything I need.' I thought of Jerome and told myself: You really are an idiot. When you get pissed, all hell breaks loose in your skull. But Big

Michel says that when you take dope, you're cool, you don't think about anything. I should have bought a dose from the Arab. So as not to hurt so much.

I'm looking for Big Michel, he's got to help me buy the remedy. Fred says he got into a car with a pair of punters. Sad is over talking with two part-timers. Sad must know where to get it; Big Michel said he used to snort from time to time. I ask Sad where I can find some smack. He says he has a connection on rue de Buci, and he'll take me over if I turn him on.

'What do you mean, turn you on?'

'You know, slip me a line. It's like a commission.'

'A line's cool. What does a dose cost?'

'A dose? Don't say that, you'll sound like a rookie. You call it a wrap. A wrap's two hundred francs.'

We're on rue de Seine, at the Aquarelle smoke shop. Sad tells me to wait on the pavement across the street. He goes in, has a long talk with a couple of Arabs. After a quarter of an hour, he comes out with one of them, a fat bloke with a face like a bulldog's: close-cropped hair, bulging eyes, tiny, widely spaced teeth, and a thick lower lip that drools on his protruding jaw. Sad introduces me.

'He's a mate, he works Saint-Germain. You can trust him, I know him.'

'Good evening,' says the fat Arab, giving me a smile that drools like his lower lip.

'This is Dani,' says Sad. 'His shit is tops. You won't be disappointed.'

The other Arab comes out of the Aquarelle, stands silently behind Fat Dani. He's got close-cropped hair too, with a scar that runs from his forehead across his

cheek down to his chin. His eyes are staring. Sad and
Fat Dani talk in Arabic together. Dani turns around and
says something in Arabic to Scarface, then asks me:

'How much do you want?'

'Two wraps.'

He says that Scarface will serve me, he's his seller,
his smack is a lot better than other places, and it isn't
cut, Dani respects his customers. So when I want
to be served, just come here to the Aquarelle, he'll
recognize me, he's got a good memory for customers.
He says good-night with a smile that makes me
want to puke. We follow Scarface from a distance.
After a dozen yards, he motions us to stop, to wait
there. He turns into a dark little street and vanishes.
Sad says he wouldn't mind knowing where Fat
Dani hides his smack, probably in some hole in the
wall. We could follow Scarface, but it would be
risky.

'Jesus, what's taking him so long?'

'It's OK. He takes a roundabout way in case the cops
are on his arse. Get your notes ready, fold them twice.
When he slips you the wraps, keep them in your hand.
If there's trouble with the filth, open your hand and
discreetly drop them.'

Scarface comes back by way of another street, walking fast. He slows down, brushes by us, the exchange
is quick, just takes a second. He says good-night and
heads for the Aquarelle. We walk toward Saint-Germain, and I give Sad one of the wraps.

'Hey, you're fuckin' nice. Really great. You shoot or
snort?'

'I snort.'

'Want to turn on together at the Drugstore?'

44

'No, I'm going to wait a bit. I'll see you later.'
'OK, later.'

I step into a phone box on rue de Rennes, roll up a
métro ticket, and unfold the wrap. The powder is dark
brown. Good Pakistani shit, Sad said. I'm hesitating, a
little afraid. I snort half the wrap, the powder stings
my nose and my eyes start to water. I wait, but the hell
inside my head is still raging, so I snort the other half.
My hands shake, warmth spreads through my body,
the powder invades my head, it feels like being pissed.
Heroin is no big deal, I tell myself, but things start
getting cool in my head. Jerome is still there, but I
don't hurt as much.

★ ★ ★

Big Michel's happy, he's made six hundred francs off
the two punters in the car. He looks at my eyes.
    'Your pupils look weird. You've been doing smack,
haven't you?'
    'I scored some off Fat Dani with Sad.'
    'What are you, stupid? Don't score off that fat pig,
his smack is crap, and it's cut like mad to boot! You've
got to score with Stéphane, his smack is tops, and when
he likes you, he'll give it to you on tick.'
    Big Michel says he'll introduce me to Stéphane
tomorrow. He also says he feels bad; he shouldn't have
told me he takes smack.
    'Stay away from that stuff. First you snort it, then
you start shooting up, and pretty soon you're hooked.'
    'Don't panic, I'll never get hooked. I won't start
shooting.'
    In my diary I write, '1 WS', for 'One wrap snorted.'

Big Michel introduces me to Stéphane the Algerian, a great-looking bloke with a face wrecked from snorting junk. He serves us in front of the building where he lives, on rue des Saint-Pères. His smack is darker and isn't as cut as Fat Dani's. I go with Big Michel who's planning to shoot up in the Decaux lavatories on rue du Four. He feels between the lavatory wall and the false ceiling for the plastic carrier with his works. He finds it and pulls it down. There are several bags of works on the false ceiling. Big Michel can tell right away if a junkie has used his works, he says: when they use someone else's hypo, they don't rinse it out; there's always blood in the syringe. I tie him off and watch him heat the smack and lemon juice in a teaspoon, stick the needle into a vein, draw up a little blood, and shoot the smack home. When he's shot it all, Big Michel stumbles, his pupils narrowed. I snort my smack; it hits faster than yesterday, warms me more. 'See how that big drive hits? This isn't the crap that fat arsehole Dani sells.'

We come out and sit down next to old Raymonde, who is begging in front of Decaux. The old lady isn't a piss-pot, just a bit cracked.

'So what were you up to in the lavatories, boys? It certainly took you long enough!'

'None of your business,' says Big Michel with a laugh. 'How are things going? Getting on OK?'

'Not bad today. It's a good neighbourhood.'

Old Raymonde counts her coins. She says she's feeling a little depressed these days, pulls her medicines from her bag: she's got stuff to sleep, stuff to wake up, stuff to feel good.

'And how are the punters? They coming through? If

46

I were younger, I'd so the same thing. Begging's not a life. Mind you, I don't sleep in the streets! I sleep in the shelters. And I'm clean! You see how clean I am?'

Raymonde gets angry and lifts up her skirt to show she isn't dirty.

'We're clean too,' says Big Michel, unfolding his big carcass. ''Bye, Raymonde!'

'Goodbye, you little tarts!'

We crease up laughing. Raymonde stinks.

Huddled in his rags, Dimitri is begging. He's been hurting since this morning and can't straighten up, he asks me for twenty francs to buy some Néocodion. I give them to him, and he drags what are left of his trainers over to the Drugstore chemist's. Pierre's sitting on a bench, a plastic carrier between his legs. He says he's knackered from a long day of filming, wouldn't mind doing a little line.

'You do commercials?'

'No, porno.'

'You do it with blokes?'

'Are you joking? With bints! Nobody buggers me!'

I try not to laugh. Big Michel told me he once saw a film that Pierre acted in. 'So I rent a porno video one day, and who do I see but Pierre, stark naked! It was set in a boarding school. Pierre shows up, it's his first day there. So the blokes at the school grab him and fuck him. Pierre pretends to scream, but by the second cock, he's moaning. Son of a bitch! All the blokes had him, there must have been a dozen of them! I've never told him I saw the film, he'd get angry. He's a good mate, so keep it to yourself!'

The punter's old and filthy; he needs a shave, and his overcoat's a sieve. He's German, I can't make out everything he's saying, but I gather he wants to take me to a hotel on Saint-Jacques, rent a fifty-franc room, and fuck me there for eighty.

'Hey, Michel, come check this out! This old geezer wants to fuck me for eighty francs in a hotel that charges fifty francs a room!'

'Did you put the screws on him?'

'I've done nothing but screw, but it's no dice. He says it's eighty or nothing.'

'Why not seventy-five fifty, you old bugger? You think this is Tati's? Shove off! In Pigalle, you can fuck for thirty. The métro's right over here!'

'Ja, ja, you good boys,' says the filthy old Hun, legging it toward the métro with Big Michel in hot pursuit, shouting that he's going to shove his cock up his arse sideways, the fucking walking corpse.

I score two wraps off Stéphane, and snort one in the Drugstore lavatories. I'll snort the other one tomorrow at quarter to twelve. Tomorrow's Wednesday, I've arranged to meet Jerome at noon in a Montparnasse restaurant, if I don't take my remedy, when I leave him, after eating and touching his hand and asking, 'Will you call me tomorrow?' and having him answer, 'All right, 'bye,' in his offhand way, I'll have a monstrous case of the blues. I'll start to cry, I'll drink beer and bad wine imagining Jerome in the baths or the lavatories somewhere, bent over, being fucked, with someone else's hands on his body. Jerome must get himself fucked on his days without children.

We order an aperitif. I can't control the shaking in my hands, my eyes must be wet and shining, my pupils staring. Jerome asks me how I feel, asks if I'm sick.

'No, not at all. I'm in great shape.'

'It's perfectly obvious you aren't all right. You're on something.'

'No, believe me, I'm not on anything.'

I'm very sick, but Jerome doesn't believe me.

'I love you. It's the first time.'

'Everybody says it's the first time.'

We got rid of a punter just in from the country, he was completely pissed, stank of liquor three yards away, said he was looking for big pricks. He asked us if we couldn't find him some blacks with huge cocks. Christian suggested he catch the first Air Afrique flight; Guy, a part-timer, called him a cunt; Big Michel hooted with laughter, saying, 'Stop, I can't stand it!' I shouted, 'Stuffed cunt,' which finished Michel off: he doubled over and puked his dope on to the pavement. Still laughing, Big Michel shouted, 'A cunt in a taxi! Driver, Cock Street, please!' I was laughing too. Cool.

★   ★   ★

My punter says he likes to plough arseholes, and he's certainly ploughing mine. He sticks a finger in, pulls it out, sticks another in, says he wants to put his whole hand in.

'All right, but you have to give me seven hundred francs.'

I get down on all fours and offer my arse. I tell the punter to grease his hand and my arse thoroughly with the genuine Chesebrough-Pond's vaseline.

49

'Be careful, it's greasy. Don't get it on the quilt.' He sticks his fingertips in, I bite the edge of the blue quilt, it feels like I'm delivering a baby backwards, I'm going to scream. I yank the punter's fingers out and shout.

'Jesus, you hurt me!' I stand up on the bed, feeling tears welling up and struggling to hold them in. The punter pulls his clothes on and yells that you don't take on this kind of work if you can't handle it, and I agreed for seven hundred francs, he's wasted his bloody time and won't give me a penny. He can take his pennies and shove them up his arse, the sodding punter with his shaved skull, his thick moustache, and that golden ring around the base of his cock, what I want is for him to get the fuck out of here. I slam the door behind him and the tears explode. But they aren't from pain or humiliation, it's something else: self-loathing. Jerome could have done it to me, he could have done anything he wanted to me, but not that bloody sod of a punter. I head down to Saint-Germain and score two wraps from Stéphane. One for each nostril.

Junk no longer blows my head off, the way it did the first time, even when I smoke it. 'Smack's a waste, when you stop feeling it,' Jean says. He and Martine shoot it up. They say that snorting's nowhere, that smack hits harder and lasts longer when you shoot. In a chemist's on boulevard Saint-Germain, I very quietly ask for a syringe.

'I'd like an insulin syringe, please.'

The woman chemist looks me over and shouts, 'One or two cc's?'

'One cc.'

She tosses the syringe on the counter as if she were

50

throwing a dog a bone. At the Drugstore, Jeannine's walking the white mongrel. I don't tell Big Michel about the spike; he'd give me hell.

Sunday, under a cloudless blue sky. I scored three wraps yesterday. Jerome is probably gardening on his hillside property. I miss him. I snort the first wrap. Jerome must be catching his train, he takes the train every Sunday at three-thirty. I prepare my works. I tighten the tie-off with my teeth, my hands are shaking, I'm a bit frightened. I dig the needle into the barely visible vein, draw up the plunger, see a spray of blood, push the plunger down, and a lump forms under my skin: I missed the vein. I have to stick the needle deeper, with the spike at more of an angle. I probe, searching for that bitch of a vein: more blood, another lump. God, I hope the smack doesn't clot in the syringe. I open and close my fist a couple of times to bring up the vein. Needle, blood, plunger, I shoot the junk: no lump, it's in my vein. I flush once and don't have time to do it again before the smack explodes in my head. It hits in a terrific rush, my neck stiffens, I feel like I'm going to keel over backwards, and I grab the white plywood table. Then it flows down, spreads throughout my body, and everything gets cool in my head. I snort the third wrap and head down to Saint-Germain, I'm not walking very straight, and I can't see the blue sky. I shouldn't have snorted the third wrap. Sitting on a bench at the bus stop, my skull feels stuffed with cotton-wool, my shirt's drenched with sweat, sweat is running down my cheeks. I need to walk. I head up to Montparnasse, toward Jerome's place. I feel sick, I can't walk anymore, I'm stumbling, but I mustn't stop walking or else I'll fall down and won't be able to get up

51

again. Jerome gets mixed up with the cotton-wool, and when I get to his street, I throw up. I walk around the block, puking as I go, as if Jerome could smell the odour of my guts. I'm puking the way a dog pisses to mark his territory. I count the pukes: eighteen. I'm hungry. It's dark, I didn't see the night fall, time has shrunk, I didn't see Jerome. I go home, swallow a piece of bread and cheese, drink a glass of water, and puke on the carpet before I can make it to the toilet. I stretch out and close my eyes; above all, I mustn't move my head. My first snort was three weeks ago. Jerome had me on the blue quilt eight months ago.

I'm falling. The night is very dark.

Big Michel ripped into me: 'You're a bloody fool, you're going to get hooked!' 'Hey, don't worry, I know where I'm going.' 'Well, it's your problem, after all . . .'

We start working together. I give him the key to my place, he gets the punters to fork out a hundred francs, the price of a hotel room, and gives them to me. It isn't exactly gracious living; I don't have much cash left, my savings are dwindling, punters are getting scarce and I need to pay for my daily wrap plus the one for the days without kids. Food is no problem: I'm not hungry anymore. The remedy has eaten away my appetite and my need to get pissed. So much the better, beer and wine on top of dope make me puke. Big Michel and Sophia have started shooting up at my place. She wants me to paint her portrait, offers me a wrap for the job. I ask for two, one this week and the other when the portrait's finished, and the stuff can't be cut. ('I'll do it in pastels. Oils would cost you ten wraps, and with your face, it would hurt my brushes too much!' 'Jesus, cut it out! Is it because of my teeth? Bloody hell, you're impossible!') We have a deal. I get the works ready. Sophia wants Big Michel to shoot her up first.

'Hang on, can't you wait a minute?'

'I always have to shoot after you. You really love me, it shows.'

'What a pain in the arse this bint is. You've got loving and shooting mixed up. You'll get your fix, dammit!'

Big Michel gets his hit, then fixes Sophia.

'It's about time you learned to shoot yourself up.'

'I can't, and you know it. I'm afraid of injections.'

'Open your eyes, dammit. What a drag you are when you've hit!'

Sophia is staggering, her lids screwed shut, mouth wide open, her stumps on display. Three spikes are lying in the fake-wood salad-bowl; I've labelled two of them 'BM Sophia' and 'Pierre'. Pierre has graduated to the spike, and now he's shooting up at my place. Big Michel says he'd like me to do a portrait of his mother when I'm finished with Sophia's. He's fond of the old lady. They all live together with his three sisters and four brothers in a housing estate out by Saint-Denis. His old man took off years ago, his mum cleans people's houses. She knows about his using smack and doesn't care. One day his sister told her that it wasn't bearable to have a junkie living under the same roof, that it was shameful to put up with, even if it's your own son. The old lady grabbed her and threw her out on the pavement, screaming, 'This is my house, and don't give me or my son grief, he can do whatever he wants to!' I agree to do the old lady's portrait for two wraps.

Saint-Germain, night-time, black pooch. Stéphane didn't come by. No remedy. My arse is dragging.

The Aquarelle, rue de Buci, rue Saint-André-des-Arts: no Fat Dani, no Scarface.

'You look fucked up,' says Big Michel.

'I don't know what's wrong with me. My stomach hurts and I feel jumpy. And I've got the blues bad.'

'That's easy. You're hurting.'

'Hey, don't shit me. Not after just a month and a half!'

'Go to the chemist's, buy some Néocodion, and take twenty of them. That should calm you down.'

I buy the Néos, swallow twenty tablets, and wait. I pick up an old punter on rue des Saints-Pères: thinning white hair, silver-rimmed glasses on a pointed nose, shifty eyes. He doesn't want to fuck, he says, just talk. He'll give me two hundred francs for a chat. 'All right,' I say, 'but we aren't going to talk about hustling.' On the Lutétia Hotel terrace, he tells me his name is Marc, that he's the dean of an engineering college. He talks about the students he's in love with: François, Robert, and the others.

'I protect them.'

'Where did you get to know them? Here in Saint-Germain?'

'No. All at college.'

'Well, you've got some nerve! You sleep with your students?'

'I'd like to, but I don't dare. But I make sure they don't fail their exams. I give them the questions beforehand. There's nothing wrong with that, is there?'

'What brings you to Saint-Germain?'

'To observe you. I enjoy meeting people, all sorts of

people. But you didn't answer me. There's nothing wrong with what I do, is there?'

'Of course not, Marc! It's kind of nice. You have to help those kids out!'

He's been observing me for an hour and a half, the Néos are doing me good, I took another twenty and with the three beers I've just drunk, I'm starting to feel better. I tell Marc about painting and about the kid-in-pain, but not about Jerome. He discreetly slips me two hundred francs and his business card.

'You're a nice boy. I'd like to talk to you again.'

'You see what time it is? We agreed on half an hour, and we've been talking for an hour and a half. You should give me something extra.'

He comes across with a hundred francs, and I promise to ring him up. In rue des Saints-Pères, I puke up the Néocodions.

Odila and Facho have nailed me in front of the Drugstore cinema.

'Let's see your papers. You new around here? Is the hustle working OK?'

'What hustle?'

'You think we're a pair of morons? What about smack? Know anything about that?'

'I don't touch that stuff.'

Facho goes off with my ID card.

'What do you do for a living?'

'I'm a painter.'

Odila gives me a strange smile.

'You work in watercolour?'

'I don't like watercolours. I don't like fluid materials.'

Facho comes back with my ID card. 'It's all right,' he says.

'Next time, you're busted. Hop it!'

We're all gathered around Fred. Dimitri has died of an overdose. Some punter found the body curled up in a cheap room in the eighteenth arrondissement.

'And the punter says, "No great loss." The bastard! He was happy enough to have Dimitri for a hundred francs!'

'Bloody sod!'

'Yeah. Are those Westons, Fred?'

'Yes. Pretty classy, eh?'

'Brill! How much they set you back?'

'Twelve hundred.'

We look at the Westons. Eric, the new boy, says he dreams of having a pair. Big Michel retorts that he'd never spend twelve hundred francs on a pair of shoes: 'You'd have to be completely cracked!' I thought of the broken-down trainers with the fallen arches that Dimitri used to slip on his dirty feet with their ruined veins.

'You're right, Big Michel. You'd have to be out of your mind.'

★ ★ ★

I'm trying to put the screws on Stéphane.

'Can you give me a wrap on tick, Stéphane? I'll pay the two hundred back this evening, I'm seeing a punter at ten.'

'You shits! You're a pain in the arse with this credit business. You know how much I'm out? A thousand.'

'I'll pay you back tonight, I swear. Christ, be a mate, my guts are hurting.'

'Big Michel owes me four hundred, Pierre two hundred. How am I supposed to buy shit if I don't have any dosh?'

'This is the first time I've asked you to carry me. You know me! I've been buying every day for the last two months.'

Stéphane gives me the wrap on credit. I couldn't find the vein in my arm so I shot up in my foot, which hurt and wasn't easy, because the vein slides around. I ran into Jerome at the Marine, was able to touch his hand and say hello. I wasn't going to meet any punter, but Stéphane didn't show up at Saint-Germain. 'You mustn't shoot up in your foot,' Big Michel said, 'the smack doesn't hit good.'

Sophia's portrait is finished. I don't get hard-ons anymore. I tried to wank off last night, thinking of Jerome, I played with my cock for half an hour but it stayed limp. This isn't the first time it's done that, even first thing in the morning. Except when I shoot up, right afterwards I get a hard-on that lasts at least five minutes. Last night I wanted to make sure: it's finished. The remedy has eaten my cock away.

★ ★ ★

The man is tall, with very blue eyes and thick lips. His right arm hangs alongside his body in a slightly curved leather sheath. The skin is waxy, the fingernails white. The arm's a corpse; it died in an accident. The man with the dead arm is a publisher, says that the kid-in-pain interests him, that he wants to publish it. We'll sign a contract, he'll give me some money when I sign, and more when the book comes out. I say yes. We sign the contract, and Dead-Arm gives me a cheque. I pay my back rent, repay Stéphane ('You've got to pay me back, or I won't serve you') and score a G, which I share with Big Michel. I buy a wallet, a purse, a watch, and a pair of very old books. I buy everything that's beautiful, nothing's too beautiful for Jerome. His birthday is in eight days.

On the phone, I wish him a happy birthday, say I have some presents for him. He says he doesn't want them, that I shouldn't have.

'If you don't want them, I'll throw them in the dustbin. It would be a pity.'

'All right. I'll stop by this evening.'

He stands motionless in the hallway, a yard from the door. I give him the curled-ribbon-silver-paper presents. He says he doesn't deserve this, I kiss him, he pushes me away.

'Don't kiss me. I stink.'

'What do you mean, you stink? I can't smell anything.'

'I don't mean smell. It's another kind of stink.'

He reads the old books, but says he can't carry the wallet, the purse, or the watch. One day, his Seiko is gone from his wrist and the gift watch has taken its place. 'You see,' he said, 'I'm trying.'

★ ★ ★

We're sitting on the rug, Sophia's bawling, she's a total mess. Big Michel has dropped her, she wants me to shoot her up with two wraps.

'Why did he drop you?'

'How do I know? He called me a stupid cow, said I was sucking all the oxygen around him, that I gave him

58

the creeps. Then he slapped me across the face. I swear, in two years it's the first time he's hit me.'

'No big deal. He'll come back.'

'Are you joking? I'm sure he's got another woman. I'm mad about that bloke. I can't live without him, d'you understand?'

'Sure I understand. Anyway, there are other fish in the sea. And what is it about him you like so much, anyway? Did he fuck you good? Is that it?'

'Are you joking? Doing smack, he couldn't even get a hard-on anymore. Well, not like before. But I don't care about that. In front, I don't feel anything anymore. Sometimes he'd . . . take me from the back, I like that better. But you swear you'll never tell him what I told you, OK?'

'I swear it! So you like going the dirt track?'

'Christ, you're vulgar!'

Sophia bursts out laughing. She wipes her snot and huddles close to me. She looks like a starved Egyptian cat. A cat skeleton.

'You'll wind up in the natural history museum, Sophia.'

'Stop, you're killing me.'

She wants to get out, go somewhere for a drink. I suggest the Marine, but only if she'll open her eyes and try to walk half-way straight.

At the Marine I order two beers. Sophia's stopped crying. She's complaining about her bad luck.

'And that medallion of the Virgin he wears around his neck, did he ever show it to you?'

'Sure, sure.'

'Well, I gave it to him. It's silver, you know! I thought that medallion was really beautiful. And when he doesn't have any dosh to score smack, who do you think buys him his wraps? Yours truly, that's who! And you think he worries about my health? My arse! He doesn't give a damn. When I told him I was going to the hospital next week to get my ovaries cleaned out, he wasn't even concerned. 'Cos, you know, I've been having pains in my stomach for a month now. Really tears me up, it hurts so much. The doc at the clinic said my ovaries were infected, that he had to operate to clean them out, but I said to myself, "If I'm not able to have kids afterwards, I'm going to overdose, I swear." If the doctor says, "You won't be able to have children anymore, Miss," I'll do a giant hit. Two Gs . . .'

'Yes, if you can't have any brats, you'll OD, you've said it twice. Christ, you're a drag tonight.'

'You're right, I'm impossible. But I feel bad. I'm unhappy, you know.'

'I know, Sophia.'

'Jesus, I'm scared about next week. But I'll take a hit before I let them cut me up.'

'Be careful, that's not too smart. Heroin and anaesthesia probably don't go well together.'

'I don't give a damn. If I don't take anything, I'll flip out!'

The beer hasn't improved matters, Sophia's eyes are spinning around like some big cartoon cat's. With difficulty, she writes out the number of the clinic so I can phone her after the operation. 'You won't let me down, will you?' She wants to take a cab to get her rotten ovaries home, so I lead her to the taxi stand outside Montparnasse station and help her in.

'When are you going to pick up your portrait?'

'After they've cleaned my ovaries. It's terrific, but you made my nose much too long, you'll have to fix it.'

'Your nose? Have you ever looked at yourself in profile?'

'Stop it, goddammit! I know I'm not the Venus de Milo, but come on!'

'OK, I'll fix it. And I'll phone you at the clinic, I promise. Remember that wrap you owe me.'

'When my ovaries are fixed!'

'You know, once your ovaries are cleaned I'm sure there's a good chance you'll still be able to conceive!'

The cab takes off.

''Bye, Sophia!'

'Ciao!'

Behind the windscreen, the Venus with rotten ovaries waves and laughs with her mouth full of stumps. Once again, I missed seeing the night fall. But I saw Sophia laugh.

★   ★   ★

Night-time, the white mongrel. Fred takes me to the Deux Magots, where Houseboat is waiting. He's a punter who doesn't want to make it with the old-timers. Fred explained why, but I don't care. Three hundred francs will buy a wrap, and I'm already into Stéphane for four hundred. Besides, I just did a hit of some white that Stéphane got in that really blows your head off. The punter is tall and thin, bald, ageless. We climb into his car in the car park and drive toward Neuilly without speaking. The quay is dark and silent. We walk up a gangplank; it's the first time I've ever been on a houseboat. Black curtains hang in front of

61

the portholes, and a black carpet covers the floor; there isn't a stick of furniture in the place. On the rug there's a bath towel, an unlabelled white glass jar and a small mirror with a razor blade, a straw, and a pile of white powder on it. Three dildos of different sizes lie in a row next to the mirror. Houseboat tells me to take off my jacket and shirt. He strips completely and gets down on all fours with his face over the mirror; he cuts the white powder into two lines, and offers me the straw.

'What is it?'

'It's coke.'

I turn him down. Cocaine isn't my thing; it makes you speedy and I want to be stoned. He sniffs a line and asks me to put the first dildo into him. I push the latex cock in, and pump it slowly in and out. He sniffs the second line and asks for the medium-sized dildo. The third one must be a foot long. Houseboat is whimpering and wiggling his arse. 'Stop!' he says. He cuts four lines on the mirror, hands me the white glass jar, and tells me to grease my hand and arm. He snorts a line and says, 'Go ahead.' I slowly twist my fingers in, push a bit to get my knuckles through. Houseboat cries out. With my hand up his arse I make a fist and twist as I push it in. Houseboat moans, lets out long 'Ohhhs', long 'Aaaahs', long 'Yesssses', then says, 'Push deeper . . .' and I push in up to my elbow. He's sniffed the four lines. I withdraw my arm, and he gives a little yelp when my knuckles come out. He stretches out on the rug, looking pained, and wanks off with his eyes closed. I look at the smeared shit on my hand and forearm; if I hadn't been loaded the smell would've make me puke. I wipe myself off while Houseboat comes, moaning. He lifts up the mirror: on the carpet lie three hundred francs, plus fifty for a cab. I feel the boat moving; I need air. Houseboat says, 'Good-night.' He never smiled, not even once. I step out on deck, and take a deep breath of the night.

★　★　★

Stéphane has suddenly disappeared, after serving us some grainy blue smack that made us throw up all evening. We rush over to the Aquarelle, where Fat Dani tells us, with his drooling smile, that he's scored some terrific white, not cut like the smack served by that amateur Stéphane who works alone, you can't work alone when you're into powder. Scarface serves us some garbage, but we don't have any choice, we don't have any other connections. We're glad Stéphane has disappeared, we owed him loads of dosh.

I ring up the clinic and ask for Sophia's room, but get the head nurse on the line instead. She asks me if I'm family. 'I'm a friend,' I say. She tells me Sophia died when she was given anaesthesia. I go down to Saint-Germain, Big Michel isn't there, hasn't shown up for three days. On the fourth he's hustling again, his blue eyes blown, says he found a connection in Montparnasse on rue de la Gaîté. We walk up rue de Rennes, talking about Sophia. Big Michel says he doesn't get it, he didn't think her heart was too weak to handle anaesthesia. Sure, there's been another woman for a long time now, but still, it really blew him away, he didn't leave his place for three days. Three days of fixes and joints.

We're on rue de la Gaîté, hurting a bit, when he says, 'That's him, the bloke over there!' He points out a short Arab, almost as broad as he is tall, with very curly,

63

almost kinky hair, and a very pointed nose: 'Saadi. His junk isn't bad.' He introduces me, and I slip the Arab a note folded in four for a wrap of white. 'This is a mate of mine,' Big Michel tells him. 'He scores every day. Will you recognize him?' 'No problem,' Saadi replies. Another one with a good memory for customers. But it isn't white, it's white brown. I don't have time to flush before my skull explodes and my neck stiffens. Big Michel gets scared. He said my eyes rolled back into my head, that I was out on my feet. I throw the 'BM Sophia' spike in the dustbin and turn the portrait with its uncorrected nose to the wall. I didn't tell Big Michel about Sophia's taking a fix before the anaesthesia. One of these days I'll have to go to the natural history museum, I'll die laughing.

I'm taking Eric, the bloke who dreams of owning a pair of Westons, to the Gaîté connection. Small and sad-eyed, with short brown hair, Eric is twenty-two but looks eighteen. He's been street-walking for three weeks. In the beginning, he says, 'I quit smack and hustling a year ago, that's all over, I won't ever go back to powder. Anyway I can't, 'cos I got cirrhosis of the liver from the lemon juice.' One evening he asked Big Michel for a connection so he could score a wrap and Michel introduced him to Stéphane. On rue de Rennes, Eric says he doesn't hit regularly, just a snort when his arse is dragging, because hustling pisses him off. He tried to work in a supermarket but that pissed him off even more, he's never been able to stand working for other people. He stops in front of a children's clothes shop, shows me a pair of white leather slippers he wants for his kid, who is three. But hey, three hundred francs

64

a pair has got to be some sort of joke, they really stick it to you with the price of clothes in this neighbourhood full of moneybags.

'All you have to do is turn a three-hundred-franc trick, and you buy the slippers.'

'Sure, but at two hundred a wrap . . .'

'You told me you weren't hitting every day?'

'Well, right now I am. Christ, am I fucking up!'

'OK, look. After your next punter, you don't take any smack and you buy the slippers. Simple, right?'

'Yes, you're right.'

I introduce him to Saadi, and Eric hands over his two hundred francs.

'He's a mate of mine, will you recognize him?'

'No problem.'

'All right, Eric, I'm going home for my hit. Catch you later.'

Eric grabs my arm, his eyes are wet. I can't believe it, is he going to start crying?

'Hey, can't you shoot me up?' he asks. 'I've never been able to shoot by myself, my girlfriend used to do it, but . . .'

'No way, man! I don't shoot up a bloke who's clean. Anyway, you know the code: You never give anybody their first fix. Ask your girlfriend!'

'She got clean six months ago and took off. Please, give me a break! I'll just do the one, and anyway I can't do any more because of my liver. If you fix me, I'll turn you on.'

'Well, OK, but you're a pain.'

He doesn't need to tie off.

'Jesus! Your veins look like motorways.'

No need to probe, the blood registers directly in the

65

syringe. Eric turns white, looks like he's going to pass out.

'Hey man, you aren't going to OD on me?'

'No, it isn't the smack, I just can't stand injections. Jesus, that's good . . . The next punter . . . I buy the slippers.'

I'm ashamed of myself. Then I hit my wrap and Eric's line and I don't feel ashamed anymore.

★ ★ ★

I'm on Gaîté, it's four o'clock, the doors to the school for handicapped children will close in half an hour. But where the hell is that bloody Saadi?

In the doorway of a tenement block in Goutte d'Or, Nina jabs the needle into the vein on her foot. We've scored a wrap on rue Myrrha and are going to share it. Saadi hasn't shown up on Gaîté for the last two days. It's a 'delivery problem', said a junkie I don't know, who also said there was plenty of dealing on rue Myrrha. Nina's pretty skinny, with eyes that may have been blue once, and straight blonde hair. She has her works in her bag, a spike we can both use. I had two hundred francs for myself, but not three francs to spare to buy a syringe.

'I don't mind your using my spike,' she said, 'but you have to shoot up after me.'

'OK, go ahead, get started.'

She crouches down while I listen intently to the sounds of doors closing, footsteps on the stairs, a woman shouting at her kids in Arabic. I don't see Nina push the plunger, but I do see her neck stiffen, her hand start to claw at her chest, her eyes widen. Her skinny body collapses, quivering. She's moaning, the spike still stuck in her foot. Nina has fallen on to the open wrap, on to *my* share of the smack. I start to scream at her: 'Jesus, you're a pain! If you aren't up to doing wraps, stick to smoking joints!'

A stain is starting to spread on her jeans between her legs. I try to salvage the rest of the junk, but it's mixed with the dirt on the floor. My guts are in torment. Nina's pissing in the filthy doorway. I step over her and leave in a rage.

We didn't know each other, we had just met that evening on rue Myrrha. She told me she'd been shooting up for ten years because of a bloke who had dumped her. 'I loved him so much, it was killing me.' She'd tried to kick the habit a hundred times and failed. The remedy had rotted her teeth; she showed me her false teeth, uppers and lowers. 'I'm thirty years old.'

I believed her. That bloke was her first sickness. The stain between her legs was an accident. An overflow.

I've lost a lot of weight, and I have dark circles under my eyes. I spend my afternoons and nights on the lookout for Saadi who isn't regular, with a bar of pain in my guts and hell in my skull. A junkie riding a moped through Saint-Germain offered to sell me a credit card for two hundred francs; he'd stolen it from some old lady by snatching her handbag. Ripping off old ladies' bags pays for his three-G-a-day habit. And I saw my old mate, a Catholic Action solicitor who lives on rue de Rennes; I used to have dinner at his place. He was out walking one evening with his two little girls, I was sitting on a bench near the bus stop, looking for a punter. 'Hello, how are you? What are you doing around here?' 'Nothing special, I'm just out for a walk.' I gave his kids a kiss. The second time, he didn't stop: 'Hi, how are you?' 'I'm fine.' I didn't have time to kiss his kids, I thought he was in a hurry. The third time he didn't say anything, just nodded. He was walking fast, too fast, keeping the girls close to him, lest I got a notion to touch them with my hustler-junkie hands, they might be contagious.

I don't know what the hell I'm doing in Saint-Germain, I don't feel like turning tricks; the punters disgust

me. I don't even think about them. All I think of are
wraps and my Gaîté connection; if it fell through, where
would I go to score my remedy? I've sunk pretty low.
I must say I really jumped in with both feet, two hits
a day, but I didn't think it would happen so fast when
I snorted my first wrap three months ago. I didn't think
I'd be stepping over Nina as she was snuffing it. I could
have called an ambulance, but all I could think about
was my smack spilled on the dirty floor. I didn't think
I'd do a first fix for a bloke who had kicked the habit
and wouldn't have shot up if I hadn't been there.

Jerome's away on his summer holiday, a month without seeing him, without touching his hand once a week.
He said he'd ring me up. I look at people on the street
and in the shops, they look normal and cool without
smack. Dimitri once told me about the Abbaye, an
outpatient clinic just around the corner where they have
shrinks who treat junkies by giving them medicine to
help them kick the habit, and if you don't have any
dosh, it's free. I want to be normal again, cool without
smack.

★   ★   ★

Friday, at the Abbaye: good morning ma'am, I take
drugs, how long have you taken drugs? Three months,
what drugs do you take? heroin, how much? in the last
month two doses a day, how do you take them? I inject
them, and why do you take drugs? well, because of a
man, yes I'm a homosexual and I'm madly in love with
him, this is the first time it's happened to me, but being
in love's a good thing, isn't it? yes, but he doesn't give
a damn and it really hurts inside, with drugs I don't
hurt so much, do you really want to quit? yes, three

69

months isn't a long time, you can do it but there isn't any miracle medicine; the medicine is you, your willpower, but I'll write you a prescription for some Seresta 50: take one in the morning, one at noon, one at night; Antalvic for the pain: two tablets in the morning two at noon two in the evening two before you go to bed, you can take more but don't take more than twelve; Mépronizine to help you sleep: one tablet half an hour before you go to bed, and above all, don't take any Néocodion, it contains codeine which is a poppy extract, it's a very weak form of the drug, that's why addicts swallow Néocodions by the handful, don't hang around the places where you used to buy drugs or visit your addict friends. Do you have a bathrub? No, well, when you start to feel bad take a very hot shower and stay under the shower as long as you can, well there you are, come and see me on Monday and if you feel that you're going to give in, don't hesitate to call me, all right thank you but I don't have any money, treatment here is free, thank you, and forget about that man, it's hopeless.

★   ★   ★

It's Saturday, and I'm feeling in the pink. I slept well, not my usual night spent between sleeping and waking, but a real night with Jerome in my thoughts when I woke up. I downed my medicine and increased the Antalvic dose. Fair weather in my guts, but I'm in a stormy mood so I treat myself to a bottle of wine I bought from the Arab on the corner who also sells fruit and vegetables. I lie down, think of Jerome who hasn't rung in three days and burst into tears. A night of medicine.

70

Sunday, there's a storm in my guts and my head, I'm in a ship surrounded by huge waves and Jerome is at the wheel. I swallow twenty Néos, curl up on the navy-blue quilt, and give up. I score a wrap on rue de la Gaîté, my hand shakes as I jab the needle into the vein on my wrist. Christ, it feels good! It must be normal to give up, tomorrow I swear I won't take anything, word of honour, just the medicine. On the Montparnasse concourse, I puke up the Néos and the medicine, but Jesus, how good I feel!

Monday, at the Abbaye: good morning ma'am, how are you? You haven't had any lapses, have you? yes, yesterday, how much? I shot a wrap, well I mean a dose, why didn't you call me? I don't know, well it's normal to backslide, it's not that important, would it be possible for you to go somewhere where you can get some sun? yes, then go and get some sun for a while, sunshine is excellent when you're going through detox, so that's settled, when do you think you'll be leaving? maybe Saturday, so let's see each other before-hand, shall we say Wednesday? all right, go and try to hold out, all right, goodbye and thank you.

The weather's fine and hot, I have forty Néos in my gut, my medicine's in my pocket. I'm going to hold out, I promise, I swear I'm not touching smack any-more. I sit down outside the Deux Magots and order a beer, letting the sun wash over me.

'What're you doing here at this hour?' Sad wants to know.

'Enjoying the sunshine.'

'Is that so? We haven't seen you at Saint-Germain for three days. Aren't you hustling anymore?'

71

'No, I'm trying to get clean.'

'Really? Too bad, I've got a great connection, the bloke deals from noon to six, so you don't get itchy. I'm heading there, want to come along?'

'Where is this connection of yours?'

'Near the Maubert-Mutualité métro station. We can walk there.'

'Well, all right.'

'But if I give you the connection, you've got to turn me on.'

'Oh, all right. Christ, what a rat you are! What's his smack like?'

'It's Paki. His wraps are pretty cut, but it's good stuff. He works alone, makes a buy in Holland every week.'

Sad's connection is leaning on a bar counter outside the Maubert métro, drinking a beer. He's an Arab, about fifty, short and squat. The whites of his bulging eyes are yellow, and he's got a protruding jaw, just like Fat Dani.

'Mehdi, let me introduce a mate of mine,' says Sad. 'He cops every day but won't give you any problems, he isn't a junkie.'

We shake hands, he says 'Hello,' and orders three beers. We talk about this and that, about the beers Mehdi drinks from morning till night – about forty of them, but he's never pissed – about the junkies who dog his tracks as soon as he shows up, one of these days they're going to get him busted, the neighbourhood's getting hot, he's going to stop serving those dossers. 'How much do you want?' he asks. 'A wrap,' I say.

'Give me your dosh discreetly.' I put the note in his hand, he slips the wrap into mine. I say, ''Bye, see you soon.' He says that if I don't find him in this bar he'll be at the tobacconist's in the street to the right, or at the second café as you go up boulevard Saint-Germain. I buy a lemon in a grocery, an insulin syringe at a chemist's. In a café I order two cups of coffee, take the spoon and lock myself in the lavatory with Sad. I give him a line. 'Christ, give me a little more.' 'You don't expect me to give you half my wrap, do you?' 'Shit, you're the one who's a rat!' 'Hey, wait a minute, man, when did you ever turn me on?' I do the hit, the wrap barely comes on.

'Bloody hell, it's garbage! You and your fucking connections! You're really a bloody sod.'

Goddam, I fucked up. And I'd sworn to myself. All right, let's say a hit from time to time, once a month. Tomorrow, I'm not taking anything.

Tuesday: medicine and Néos. Jerome phones, everything's fine at the white house, there's the lawn to mow and the copper pots to polish. He'll ring me again in a couple of days; with his parents around it isn't easy to get away to telephone. His voice affects me as much as three boxes of Néocodions, and I start thinking about him. I don't even have a photo of his sad, round eyes, his thin, straight nose, his curved lips . . . and then the blues hit me like a ton of bricks. I score a wrap on Gaîté. This one really is the last.

Wednesday: at the Abbaye. good morning, well? I guess I'm OK, no lapses? Er, yeah, a little hit yesterday, a what? an injection, all right, let's not have any more lapses are you taking your medicine? yes, yes, in a week we'll cut down on the dosage, there's no point in getting free of one drug only to get hooked on others that

73

happen to be medicine, all right, so are you having any problems with diarrhoea or constipation? no no, I'm pretty regular, when will you be back from your trip? July the fifteenth, and where are you going? to the Auvergne with some friends, ah, the Auvergne is very pretty, I'm told, I've never been there, so let's see, you say the fifteenth, so what do you say we see each other on the seventeenth? the seventeenth would be perfect, all right, see you the seventeenth, and hang in there, yes yes, goodbye and thank you.

Thursday: medicine and Néos. Jerome rings up, it's easier on Thursdays, when his parents go shopping. Néocodion blues. That evening I score a wrap, but it's absolutely the last one. Half a wrap today, the other half tomorrow, then on Saturday, it'll be the Auvergne, four days of fresh air and I'll get clean. Anyway, I'm going to the country without any smack and I won't be seeing Stéphane, Fat Dani, Mehdi or Saadi. When I come back I'll start writing another book; I'll write the story of the kid-in-pain's mother. Why not?

Saturday: I take a double dose of medicine, pack ten boxes of Néos in my suitacse, write a big 'C' for 'Clean' in my diary and circle it. I'm leaning against the wall outside my building, the two Seresta tablets have turned my head to mush. Sylvette and Jean-Pierre and their blue-eyed, golden-haired son David are coming to get me in their car in front of my place. I squat down, my suitcase between my legs.

The Auvergne turns out to be black: black mountains, black houses, a black church a few yards from Sylvette and Jean-Pierre's place. I slept in the car on the way, knocked out by the medicine. When we got to the country we bought bread, sausages and rosé wine.

Jean-Pierre barbecued the bangers on a grill in his little corner of uncleared land, Sylvette prepared the rooms, David rolled in the grass, and I swallowed ten Néos with my rosé.

I didn't get a wink of sleep, what with the bloody church's electric carillon ringing the hours and half-hours day and night. I lay on the bed, eyes open, a cigarette in my mouth, with Jerome; whatever possessed me to follow him into the lavatories in that shopping centre?

That afternoon, we went to visit an old castle. It was hot as blazes. 'You'll see,' Sylvette whispered in my ear, 'things will get better. You'll get your health back here. We love you.' A steep climb to the castle, with people dressed up like in the Middle Ages greeting the tourists and speaking the way they used to, in old French. Two knights duelled with swords as three-year-old David marvelled. At the castle souvenir shop, Jean-Pierre bought him a plastic knight in black armour carrying a lance, sitting on a white horse. David got sleepy. The sun flooding through the car window made us drowsy, and he lay his sweaty blond curls on my lap. I stroked his head and he fell asleep. I had fifty Néos in my stomach and felt like puking but controlled myself so as not to wake him. That night, we ate sausages and drank rosé. I downed twenty Néos, one Mépronizine, and went to bed with Jerome. Next day was 14 July, Bastille day.

There wasn't any dance-hall in town, so we took the car and drove some twenty kilometres out into the sticks. There were rides for the kids, shooting galleries, candy floss, and a plywood hut with a bar and a wooden floor to take a spin on. Lots of drunken meat on display.

At the bar, I knocked back five beers and twenty Néos – I had already swallowed fifty of them. Outside, kids were setting off firecrackers, so I stepped out of the hut. The air smelled of gunpowder and the first rocket shot off into the blue-black sky, falling back in a burst of coloured sparks. More rockets rose, and with each burst I felt a terrific kick in the ribs, an incredible spasm of anxiety. David was riding on his father's shoulders, saying 'Oh, daddy!' every time a rocket burst. I went behind the hut and puked up my seventy Néos, wondering what the fuck I was doing there. I started to cry, it did me good. All right, I said to myself, tomorrow we head back to Paris, we'll leave early so as not to get caught in traffic, we should be there about six, I'll drop off my bags at my place and rush to Gaîté and score a super-wrap.

Wednesday, at the Abbaye: good morning ma'am, oh! how well you look, so how was your stay in Auvergne? it was fine, you haven't had any lapses have you, I hope you behaved yourself, no problem, good, have you had a blood test? no not yet, aren't you afraid of AIDS? no, to tell you the truth I don't give a damn, whether I die of that or something else, you seem quite resigned, no, no, but I'm a fatalist we don't choose our destiny, I think you're wrong, we may not choose our origins but as far as our destiny, that we do choose, we influence it, yes ah, well how do you feel? very well, I'm fine, in that case we're going to reduce the treatment, cut out the Antalvic, here's a prescription; shall we see each other in two days? all right, go on it's nothing but a bad memory now, goodbye, goodbye and thank you.

That's right, madam shrink! And what about Jerome?

76

Doesn't she have a cure for that? I didn't tell her about the super-hit I had last night, that was really something! Any more than I told Dimitri that I knew his lady shrink, my 'friend' the Catholic Action solicitor's wife. There probably wasn't much of a crowd behind Dimitri's hearse. I wonder if they planted him with his rotten trainers on. See you never, madam shrink!

That does it, I'm not getting clean, smack's just too good, but I'm limiting myself to one wrap a day. The man with the dead arm will give me money in September when the kid-in-pain comes out, but I have to find some dosh in the meantime. I telephone Marc, tell him I'm in a jam: 'I'm getting a cheque one of these days and I don't hang out in Saint-Germain anymore, can you lend me a hand?' We arranged to meet at the Coupole, we talk about his students, about the one who flew to New York to work on Wall Street; Marc is unhappy, he was his favourite. I don't give a damn, it's eight o'clock, and that slight pounding in my guts is starting up, it's time for my remedy. He hands me the money, says he's happy I'm not spending time in Saint-Germain, that I'm doing other things, painting and writing. 'You're right, Marc. Well, 'bye, I'll be seeing you.'

Big Michel, Pierre, and two blokes I didn't know came to shoot up at my place. There were four labelled syringes in the fake-wood salad-bowl, and my watch was lying on a shelf behind the white plywood table. After the blokes shot up and left, my watch had disappeared. This week, there are two 'JTs' in my diary above the 'I W'. Only two. Like last week.

Gaîté has become the pits, you have to hang out for hours to get served, but Saadi says there'll be a seller soon, and dealing will be more regular. I accept a commission for a portrait of an old lady with blind eyes and parchment skin, wearing a white blouse: an oil painting, dark-blue background, payment on completion. I pick up my brushes, the lady's ninety-eight, she'll wind up in my veins. Powdered. Brown or white.

I stuff my book collection into a big plastic carrier: Genet, Duras, Dostoevsky, paperbacks and hardcovers, but not *Painters of Happiness*. Pierre tipped me off that you can sell books at Gilbert Jeune's place. I'm waiting at Gilbert's with my books piled on the counter. A bloke's standing next to me, wearing a sweater and coat in spite of the August heat. He's tall, about thirty, just skin and bones, I've never seen a bloke so skinny. He's leaned a guitar against the counter, and has a suitcase full of old books out on the top. 'Are you selling so you can score, too?' he asks.

'How can you tell?'

'The needle tracks on your wrist. A blind man could spot them.'

He discreetly pulls up the sleeve of his coat and displays a line of scabs running from his wrist to the inside of his elbow. He says his name's Frank, he plays the guitar in the métro or on hotel terraces, sleeps in a cellar in Bagneux, and stole the suitcase from another cellar he broke into. He wants to know if I've got a connection in the area. It's only one o'clock, and apart from Mehdi I don't know anywhere else to score so early. I don't even know whether I'd even recognize him, I just met him once, but we can give it a try. It'll depend on how much they give us for the books.

A hundred and forty francs for me, twenty for Frank.

'Christ, what bastards!'

'Fuck, you're a clod! You could have stolen some fancier books!'

'Your Arab won't sell us a wrap for a hundred and sixty, will he?'

'I can try to bring him round.'

Frank chucks the suitcase into the Seine and we make the rounds of the bars around Maubert-Mutualité, but Mehdi's not there. Frank says he's got a connection of his own, but it's in a café out by Père-Lachaise. He's a retired burglar who's turned to dope, but only white brown, and not every day. We make for Père-Lachaise, with Frank talking a mile a minute. He talks about smack and speedballs, a mixture of heroin and coke: 'It's the big steel-blue metal pinball, man.' And when he passes a woman with a nice body, he starts raving.

'Son of a bitch, I'm hallucinating! Oooh, she's a dolly, that one! I've got a hard-on like a donkey's dick. Oh, the bitch! I wouldn't mind giving her some, shove it right up her.'

'Have you finished talking rot? In the state you're in, can you even get a hard-on anymore?'

'What? Me, man? Mine's hard all the time!'

'Sure, sure.'

I give Frank my dosh and he goes into the café while I wait under a tree with his guitar. ('If you pull a fast one, I'm taking it with me,' I told him.)

By the time he comes out half an hour later, I am about to scarper with his guitar. He says he managed to score for the hundred and sixty. We nick a lemon from a grocery stand, rummage through a dustbin for a Coke tin to heat the powder in. I've got three francs

80

left to buy a spike with. Frank's HIV-positive, so I'll shoot first. We can find water at the Père-Lachaise cemetery.

We're walking along the cemetery pathways, looking for a big, cosy vault. We pass the memorials to the concentration camp deportees: Ravensbruck, Mauthausen, Auschwitz. I stop short in front of the Büchenwald memorial, struck dumb by the statue: three tangled, emaciated bodies, their heads lowered, screaming, a jumble of bronze bones.

'Christ, what's keeping you?' asks Frank.

'I don't know. It just overwhelmed me, I don't know why.'

'Hey, man! This is no time to be wanking your brain. I've got a monster cramp right here, above my cock, and only smack will wank it away. Come on!'

We find a comfortable crypt in the old part of Père-Lachaise.

'Hello, you stiffs! Mind if we do a little hit?' Frank shouts.

'Shut up, goddammit! You'll have a guard on us!'

A vague warmth; the smack is garbage. Frank looks loaded. We head back down the paths, with Frank walking in slow motion, lifting his legs very high.

'What are you playing at?'

'Shhh! Mustn't wake the dead . . .'

He's hungry, hasn't eaten since yesterday evening. At Montparnasse we split a piece of bread and cheese, he eats while talking about women and his stiff cock. I'm not listening, I'm elsewhere. In Buchenwald.

A single 'JT' Sunday at nine thirty. I sold two large paintings to pay my rent. Saadi's found his seller,

81

Carlos, a Portuguese ('but from an Algerian cock,' said Big Michel, referring to his pock-marked face). The kid-in-pain is off the presses, with an elegant grey cover and my name in black letters. I don't feel any emotion, I'm just thinking of the cheque the corpse-bearer is going to give me.

On Gaîté, I run into Abdel and Francine, his woman. When they shot up at my place one day, they sat their one-year-old on the carpet, the kid started to bawl, Francine picked him up and Abdel fixed her in the hand while Francine rocked the kid, saying, 'I know you're hungry, sweetheart, we're going to go home, but wait until Daddy's finished with my hit.' I ask Abdel if he's seen Pockface. No, he hasn't seen him. 'I'm heading down rue Montparnasse,' he says, 'then I'll walk back up to the Liberté. If you see him, tell him to wait for me there.' Avenue du Maine, rue Vandamme: no Pockface. On rue de la Gaîté, Abdel's standing in front of the Liberté with Francine and two blokes. I say, 'So, did you see Pockface?' He doesn't know what I'm talking about, he answers. 'I'm with these two police officers . . .' One of the cops, a big husky bloke in a ski anorak, pulls out his badge.

'You looking for the dealer, too?'

My legs start to shake.

'What dealer? Pockface is a mate, we had arranged to meet.'

The copper points an index finger to his forehead. 'You think I've got "clod" written here, you fucker?'

The other cop drags Abdel into the entrance to a block. Ski Anorak tells me to raise my arms, and says to Francine, 'Hop it, you.' He searches my pockets,

82

opens my pack of Marlboros, unscrews my cigarette holder, shows me the filter:

'What's this?'

'It's a filter to trap the tar.'

He throws it away, pats my body through my clothes, feels my balls.

'You have anything in your pants?'

'Sure. A pair of balls.'

'Don't try to score off me, arsehole, or you'll find yourself in deep shit.'

This has got to be the first time I haven't been in the mood to play with a bloke who's feeling my balls. 'All right,' he says, 'that'll do. Clear off. And don't get caught around here this evening, there's going to be a raid. I'm just giving you a tip . . .'

Abdel is pale with rage, he says the fucking cop made him drop his trousers, lift his balls, and spread his cheeks, just in case he had a wrap stuck to the hair of his arse!

'He asked me, "You take drugs?" I told him I never touched the stuff. These cops are real fools; it didn't even occur to him to make me roll up my sleeves!'

A call from Jerome, he'll be back tomorrow, he's feeling rested from a holiday spent reading, gardening and walking. We could get together the day after tomorrow for lunch, he says, meet on the place du Châtelet around half past twelve. I have to find four hundred francs tomorrow to score my evening wrap and the one for tomorrow morning.

'Hello, mum? It's me . . . Yes, yes, I'm all right, well, no, not really, I have a problem, I'm in a jam, I don't have a penny to buy something to eat . . . Well, yes, I know, if you could give me a hand . . . Well, five hundred, if you could . . . OK, fine, I'll be waiting for you.'

I ate with Jerome in a restaurant in les Halles, it was cool, I was feeling loose. He had to stop by the school to take care of some paperwork. I went with him, wanted to kiss him in his office, he pulled back, said, 'No.' I insisted, I put my tongue in his lifeless mouth; I couldn't find his tongue but was still able to swallow a little of his saliva.

The cheque from the man with the dead arm came through with two or three good reviews of the kid-in-pain in the press. My birthday was 18 October. Jerome knew about it, but didn't say anything. 'JT.'

'My birthday was a week ago.'

'Yes, I knew. But I didn't want to wish you a happy birthday.'

'Well, why not?'

'I just didn't want to. You know why.'

'No, I don't. I don't get it, it's idiotic. Stupid and cruel. Oh well . . .'

It was an odd place, a strange house I had never seen before, I climbed a few steps to a little balcony, it was night outside, I lay down on the balcony in front of the door and waited. The door opened, there was light behind the door, a very bright light, a man I didn't know appeared in the light. A voice behind the man, behind the light, said, 'Don't worry, I know him. Let him sleep there if he feels like it, he isn't bothering anyone.' It was Jerome's voice. The door slammed shut. I had come to the balcony to wait for Jerome, to see him, I didn't know that he was inside with another

man. Curled up on the balcony, I knew that the man
in the light was Paris-Tokyo. It was six in the morning
after a bad dream, and I was feeling as gloomy as I ever
get. I opened the fridge, took out the little clear plastic
container I store the filters from my fixes in, put them
in a spoon, added water and lots of lemon juice, and
started probing for my vein at six-thirty in the morning.

At noon, I was pushing through the door of the bar
where I had met Mehdi. I looked at the men at the
counter, didn't recognize Mehdi, couldn't remember
his face, so I went to the other places he'd told me
about. In the one on the right as you go up boulevard
Saint-Germain a bloke with a moustache was sitting at
the counter in front of a beer. 'Is that you, Mehdi?' I
asked. 'What do you want with Mehdi?' he asked. 'You
a cop?' I said I wasn't a cop, that I had met Mehdi in
the other café 'down there', I had been with Sad.

'I'm Mehdi,' he said, 'what do you want?'

'I'd like a wrap.'

'How do I know you aren't a cop? I don't remember
you with Sad.'

Under the counter, I discreetly pulled up my jean
jacket sleeve and showed him the fresh scabs on the
veins in my wrist.

'OK, all right. You scared me. I figured you were a
cop. You don't look like a junkie.'

He bought me a beer, said he was careful about cops,
he'd sniffed out two or three in the neighbourhood who
knew him well because he used to be a burglar. He'd
spent fifteen years in the nick. The first time, he got
ten big ones for a bank job; the second time, five for a
jewellery store.

'You know, it's funny, I'm the only one in my family

85

to turn out badly. My father's a doctor in Algiers, I have two brothers in Paris, a solicitor and a doctor. But I'm all set now. Junk is mellow. And I don't make people take drugs, they're the ones who come to buy it from me.'

'Follow me,' he said, and I followed him down to the cellar, where the bar's lavatories are. He slipped me the wrap. 'Thanks,' I said, 'and thanks for the beer. See you tomorrow.'

Next day, Mehdi didn't offer me a beer, just said, 'Come with me.' In the cellar, he pulled out a gun and stuck the barrel in my stomach. I felt the heat rush to my head, started to sweat. 'I got held up by two blokes yesterday,' he said, 'I had ten Gs on me, it's . . .' We heard footsteps, a woman was coming down the stairs. With the gun, Mehdi pushed me towards the stalls, muttering 'Pretend you're taking a piss' through his buck teeth. I leaned against the urinal without pulling my cock out, feeling the weapon pressed against my lower back. I could hear the woman making a phone call. In a daze, I was thinking it must be a mistake, and then I thought maybe I'd got him into trouble. But who could have pulled a stunt like that? I never caused anybody any trouble. Meanwhile the woman wouldn't stop talking. When she left, Mehdi grabbed me by the collar, spun me round, and jammed his gun back into my guts.

'Very curious, isn't it? Yesterday, you show up. I don't know you, but I serve you anyway. An hour later, two blokes rip me off. Don't you think that's strange?'

'You must be mad! I don't see the connection! Yesterday I told you I was a mate of Sad's. Ask him if he knows me, you'll see, he'll tell you I'm no robber. Anyway, it wouldn't have been too smart for me to stick you up. Think about it. Would I have come back to score?'

Mehdi mulled that over for a few seconds, than let go of my collar and stuffed his gun into the waistband of his trousers, under his shirt.

'All right, I believe you. I'm sorry, it's just that I really thought you sent those two sods to rob me.'

He said he knew one of them, a handsome-looking junkie, and that he'd find him. He wouldn't kill him, he said, but he knew what he was going to do to him. When he was finished, he wouldn't be showing his handsome face; even his mother wouldn't recognize him. 'It's his tough luck, he was only doing what he was told, but I won't give him a break. Too bad, he's a young bloke.' He was spluttering as he spoke, I took out my handkerchief and wiped my brow, thinking I needed a good hit. Mehdi served me, and I shakily slipped him my folded notes.

'Again, I'm sorry. Forget it.'

'Easy. I stick the needle in, and I forget.'

I buy a hundred-page Clairefontaine spiral notebook and start the story of the kid-in-pain's mother. She'll be the one to tell the story: about growing up in Vendée, days of poverty, potatoes without meat, the war and the exodus, falling head over heels in love with a handsome drunk who'll rip her vagina on their marriage night. She'll tell about her ripped belly, about her flesh cut open for the birth-cry of her first kid and then the birth-cry of her second, about the handsome drunk's death in a vomit of blood and cheap wine.

She'll show her photos of Vendée, of the exodus, of the handsome drunk, of her kids, and she'll say: 'Here it is. It was like this.' The handsome bloke died forty years ago. She'll say she still loves him.

My diary reads '½ W' for Monday at eleven thirty, '½ W' for Friday noon, and '1 W' every evening of the week. I sell three 14-carat-gold rings by weight, gifts from the man who didn't commit suicide.

Jerome and I ate dinner not far from the Opéra. I wanted to take the bus home, so we took the bus that runs from the Opéra to Montparnasse by way of Saint-Germain-des-Près. It stopped in front of the Drugstore, where Fred was pacing the pavement.

'Well, what do you know,' said Jerome, 'it's Fred.'

'You know him?'

'Yes, I've gone with him a couple of times.'

Every day of the week, in the morning section, I've written '½ W'.

I sell three more rings. I've been waiting for hours, and there's no sign of Pockface, I'm leaning my wasted body against the grillwork at the Edgar-Quinet métro exit. On the other side of the intersection, a girl is standing under the neon lights of a self-service launderette, waiting. A girl dressed all in black.

III

I phone Ida, who says she's dragging. She's barely been able to haul herself out of bed these last days, and opening the shop and putting out the stock is hell; she feels like she's sixty years old and weighs two hundred pounds. 'I hope I make a sale at the shop today,' she says, 'because I need two hundred for tonight and the bloody customers pay for everything by cheque. They even write a cheque for some fifty-franc trinket.' I tell her I've got a little money, I can score for both of us tonight, and tomorrow, she can score for us. Far out, she says.

We team up. I score one night, she scores the next, and on the third we share our Néocodions.

She tells Pockface I've written a book, and he wants a copy of the kid-in-pain, with a dedication. On the first page, I write, 'For Carlos. This story in black and white.' Now when I score, I slip my dosh between the pages of the kid-in-pain.

One evening, I'm hurting badly and I've got a hundred-franc note folded in four in the palm of my hand. I want Pockface to serve me half a wrap, but he refuses, so I tell myself I'd better lay it on thick, that I'll have to cry. My gut is hurting so bad, crying should be easy.

I beg, tell him it's the first time I've ever asked for half a wrap, I know he doesn't usually do that, but Christ, I buy from him every day. Then I start to bawl, say that I'm at the end of my rope, that I'm going to snuff it right then and there. 'Here, I'll give you my watch, you want it?' He isn't interested in the watch, it isn't gold, so he can't sell it, and anyway, the decision isn't up to him, he'll have to ask Saadi. 'Wait for me here.' I wait near the Gaîté métro, my hands on my stomach to warm it, blurred visions of powder in my head. Pockface returns and says all right, but he has to go to a café lavatory to prepare the half-wrap. He comes out of the place, and slips me a skimpy wrap. I rush home, shoot it up. It barely eases the pain. I telephone Ida.

'So have you sold anything?'

'Fuck all,' she says. 'If I don't make a sale, I'll steal the change from the cash register and figure out some way to pay it back tomorrow.'

I telephone Alain, the punter with the fancy bank job. 'I'm in a jam,' I tell him. 'I'm expecting a cheque any day now, can you help me out?' 'I'll lend you five hundred,' he says, 'but you have to pay it back soon. I'll trust you.'

'Can you imagine that, Ida? I ask a punter for five hundred and I have to pay him back! The world's upside-down!'

At six o'clock, I run into Ciel.

'What the hell's Carlos up to?'

'He isn't coming. He got busted.'

'Shit! Was he carrying much?'

'Thirty-six grams.'

'Bloody hell!'

'But Saadi's going to get him the best solicitor. He won't hang him out to dry, and Carlos would never grass on Saadi.'

'Christ, what are we supposed to do for smack?'

'There'll be another seller, but it'll take a few days. Don't worry. Saadi wouldn't leave you without junk.'

'An Arab is taking advantage of the situation and is selling smack at the Gaîté métro,' says Abdel, who just scored. He points out the dealer to me, and I walk over to him. He's just served a junkie wearing a pair of checked trousers, a three-day beard hiding his sunken cheeks and toothless mouth; we know each other by sight. 'Don't bother,' the junkie says, 'there's nothing left, I just scored the last two. But there'll be more in an hour, for sure.' I offer to buy a wrap from him. If he hits one wrap, he'll be able to hold out for an hour, but I can't, I'm hurting too much. 'I'll see,' he says. 'If it's righteous stuff, I'll sell you one, if it's garbage I'm shooting both of them.' On rue de l'Ouest, he hits me up for three francs to buy a spike; in a grocery store he picks up a litre of water, a tin of fruit juice so he can use the lid for a spoon, and says, 'Pay up.' I ask him if he thinks I'm an idiot, he answers that if I pay he promises to turn me on for free, even if the stuff is garbage.

On the first-floor stairs of an old building on rue Vercingétorix, the junkie unpacks his works and tells me to keep an eye out. With my guts on fire, I stand watch in the ground-floor hallway. Five minutes go by. I climb the stairs, the junkie has shot up the first wrap, his eyes are glassy, he's stiff as a board. 'So?' I ask. 'Is it any good?' The smack is garbage, he answers, he has to take the second wrap. He's mumbling, his gestures vague. This fucker's loaded, I think, he's going to shoot the second wrap and I'll be whistling for my hit. My foot lashes out and catches the junkie full in the face; his cheekbone cracks and he collapses on the stairs without a sound, blood dripping along his cheek. I scoop up the wrap and race out, laughing, thinking that the people in the building will call an ambulance, that the cops will find him with his spike in his arm, that this is one fucking arsehole junkie who's going to get a hell of a surprise when he wakes up.

I don't tell Ida that I scored some white for free that got me really ripped.

Ida's feeling good this morning, she shot her filters before leaving for work and got some good juice out of them. It set her right up, she was even singing as she put out the merchandise. Saadi's found a seller named Joao, a Portuguese junkie who always has his woman, Claudine, in tow. Joao deals from two o'clock on, you meet him at the Pomme d'Api, a bakery on boulevard Montparnasse. So we gather there, a dozen of us, all sick, waiting for Joao and Claudine to come out from wherever they're shooting up.

In two months, I've covered twenty pages of the Clairefontaine notebook. The writing hasn't come easily. I set out to score my remedy every day at two o'clock. If I don't have my morning fix, after a cup of tea and a shit, I can't write a line. I show the twenty pages to the man with the dead arm, and he offers me a contract with an advance twice that he gave me for the kid-in-pain. I'll get the first instalment when I sign, the second when I reach a hundred pages, the third when I turn in the manuscript. We sign the contract, and the man hands me a cheque.

The Christmas‑tree‑tinsel‑lights‑streamers‑and‑paper-hats holidays are coming up, so I buy three silk ties, in reds and blues. For Jerome.

'Was that you I saw on television the other evening,' asks Mehdi, 'with the bloke who hosts that programme on books?'

'Yeah, that was me.'

'Christ, I couldn't believe my eyes. I kept telling myself, that couldn't be my customer. You looked pretty cool.'

'Well, that's bloody amazing, 'cos I was totally loaded when I got to the studio! I did a super-hit at three o'clock and drank a lot of wine with my publisher. But you couldn't tell I was wasted?'

'Not at all.'

I get a registered letter from my landlord: I have six months to pack my bags and clear out.

Christmas holiday in the white house, three 'JTs' in my diary, and 'POJ' for Monday, 28 December when I posted him the three silk ties. When he got back, he gave me an elegant brown and black Pierre Balmain cigarette holder. I went to the school with him and managed to steal a little of his saliva.

Pierre comes to my place to shoot up, and I ask him for news of Big Michel, who hasn't been around Gaîté. He tells me Michel's scoring somewhere else, over by l'Odéon. As we chat while preparing our works, Pierre

95

tells me he's HIV-positive and that it freaks him out to have that shit in his blood.

'Are you careful with the punters?'

'I don't give a damn. Last night, over by Dauphine, I fucked a woman, her husband wanted me to fuck her in their car while he had a wank, and I shot my load into her twat.'

'Jesus! You might have put on a condom!'

'I didn't have one. And anyway, all they had to do was pick up a bloke with a condom.'

Pierre shot up on one of his forearm motorways and the blood started to spurt when he withdrew the needle. He went into the kitchen, turned on the tap, and ran the water on his arm, over the dirty washing-up.

'Bloody hell, you're really disgusting! You just told me you're positive and here you are bleeding all over my washing-up!'

'Oh, for Christ's sake, take it easy. Just use a little bleach. And anyway, you share your spike with Ida.'

'Sure, but Ida doesn't share with anyone!'

'Are you going to tell me you've never shot up after Big Michel?'

'So what? What business is it of yours? I've never made you shoot up after me, have I?'

'Jesus, you're jumpy! In the beginning, you were cool, but now you're too speedy. I don't recognize you.'

'I know. It's the fucking dope. I feel it less and less.'

There's an odd smell in the flat, like somebody's feet. Ida is sitting across from me, preparing her hit.

'Don't you think it smells strange in here?'

She sniffs the air.

'No, not really. I don't smell anything.'

I bend over, look at Ida's feet under the plywood table. She's taken off her shoes, and her feet are black with grime.

'You're the one who's smelling! Look at your feet! When was the last time you took a shower?'

It's been three days since she last washed, three days since she's gone home to her Moroccan. Didn't feel like it, she says. She's been wandering around looking for a connection, looking for credit, then sleeping the rest of the night in the métro. I tell her to take a shower after she hits. The plastic shoes make her feet sweat, she explains.

No Joao, no Claudine. They usually sleep in cellars or car parks but last night they took a room in a hotel in the neighbourhood, some junkie told me, but nobody knows which one. I decide not to hang around. One of these days we're going to get busted; you never see the filth but they're everywhere. You really have to be a clod to deal out of a bakery, I think. Heading up Gaîté, I see a woman coming the other way, pushing a bicycle. She has short brown hair, a pretty face, hazel eyes that look loaded. 'Hello,' she says, using my first name. 'Don't you recognize me? I'm Séverine.'

She's speaking low and very slowly. I don't remember her but I pretend to. 'You don't look well,' she says. 'Are you hurting?'

'Starting to, a bit. In an hour, it'll be hell.'

She has a connection, she says, an Arab who is squatting in a building on rue Daguerre. The smack's yellow and grainy, but it's tops.

'Everybody says theirs is tops.'

'Word of honour. Look at my eyes; don't I look loaded?'

I look at her eyes. She's loaded, all right.

'I'm so stoned I can't even get on my bicycle.'

As we walk down Daguerre, Séverine tells me about Saadi and how he protects Ciel. She lives with him, does the cleaning, cooks meals, does the washing-up and the shopping. Saadi beats her from time to time, sometimes really hurts her, but she doesn't say a word. Saadi gives her smack, and at three Gs a day, she can't complain.

We're in a smelly room with an old bed covered with a blanket spattered with stains and spots, a low table, a television set, and pin-ups of naked women on the walls. There's no daylight; the windows are covered with blankets, and a bedside lamp perched on a second television set dimly illuminates the room. An old Arab is sitting on the edge of the bed. Séverine tells him I'm a friend, not a cop, that I score every day like clock-work, that he can trust me. The old man looks at me and says, 'Sit down, brother.' He asks me what I want. 'A half,' I say. He pulls a parcel wrapped in newspaper from a plastic carrier: it's his smack. He serves me, and I snort a line. I don't feel anything, but that's not surprising: snorting no longer has any effect on me. He gives Séverine a super-hit, and I wonder what this girl is doing with the old Arab. Why is he turning her on for free? It doesn't seem to be on credit. I shake the old man's hand. 'Come back whenever you like,' he says, and walks with me to the door leaning on a cane. I give Séverine my phone number. She tells me that if I want the smack to really hit, I have to add some spirits to

98

the spoon, but just a few drops, and only when the lemon juice is hot.

I crush the yellow lumps and shoot up a good-size line. Nothing. I put the rest of the half in the spoon, heat it, add a few drops of spirits, and shoot. It doesn't come on, and there's no rush. The pain blurs a little, but I've blown four hundred francs. I hope to God Ida's made some sales.

Gold and Dental Fillings Bought and Sold. In a jewellery store near the Opéra, I sell my gold Dupont lighter for twenty francs. I have a some gold presents left – a cross, a gold chain, and a Cartier bracelet – but those aren't for sale.

On the Montparnasse tower concourse last night, three junkies robbed Joao and Claudine of four bags of smack, twenty wraps' worth. They were heavies from another part of town, says Claudine shakily. But Saadi didn't believe them, said they aren't selling for him anymore and that they had to pay for the twenty wraps. That's twenty times two hundred francs, makes four thousand francs, less the thirty per wrap he gave Joao as a commission. 'We're in deep shit! We owe three thousand, and don't have a penny . . .'

'And we shot a half-wrap every day, that bastard made us pay for our stuff.'

'We've got to scarper, and fast!'

For the last three days, Mehdi's been nowhere to be found. His smack is worthless, but scoring at noon, even if it's garbage, can save a bad morning. Fat Dani's been busted too, but the cops let him go the next day.

Dani and Mehdi hate each other, so some people think he grassed on Mehdi in exchange for his freedom.

★　★　★

'Ida, you have no idea how much I miss Jerome. I can't stand it.'

'Oh really? Jesus, I've got a pain in my stomach. Anyway, why do you like him so much? Is he good in bed?'

'He's a god. But that isn't all of it. I just miss everything about him.'

'What about dope? Doesn't he say anything about that?'

'No. He doesn't care, I think . . . I don't know. But that's just the way it is. If I didn't love him, it wouldn't matter what he did, I wouldn't give a fuck. Anyway, he never tells me what's on his mind, so he isn't going to start now.'

'I don't get it. He doesn't love you, but you go on seeing him.'

'I know, it's stupid. But I can't live without him. I go to sleep thinking about him, and I think about him when I wake up.'

'Can't you just tell him, "It's all over, we aren't seeing each other anymore?" '

'Yeah, that would just suit him down to the ground. Since he's stopped screwing me, he must think I'm a pain in the arse. It can't be much fun to fool around with a bloke you don't love. Maybe he pities me . . . That must be it; he pities me.'

'I've got to leave you now, here comes a customer. Maybe I'll make a sale. See you.'

100

One day, he said I was running away. That smack was an escape into the future.

★ ★ ★

The old Arab's stuff may be garbage, but it can't be helped. I can't hold out, so I rush over to rue Daguerre. I'll wait for Séverine and persuade her to get the Arab to give me some smack on tick.

The old man says Séverine should show up any minute. 'Sit down,' he says. I sit on the bed next to him. He has a sparse white moustache, thick lips that part in an unhealthy smile to reveal a fortune in gold teeth. He says he's a Kabyle, talks about Kabylia, I'm having trouble following him, my skull is in my guts and my guts are burning up. Pointing to a pin-up of a naked woman with enormous breasts, he says that's the way he likes them, with big tits and fat arses. He feels between his legs and says he's got a hard-on, that at sixty-five his erections are as stiff as ever. He lays his hand on my thigh and strokes it gently. He says he has a woman over there, back home, but that she's 'like this', showing me his cane; she's as dry as a stick of wood. I ask him when Séverine is coming, if she's coming at all. His lips reveal his gold teeth and he answers that she isn't coming. I get it, then. I tell him that I'm hurting, that I need my remedy right away but that I don't have any dosh; that's why I had to see Séverine, I was hoping she could help me. He says it's no problem, we can work something out. He draws closer. I can smell his breath, it stinks of onions. I raise my thigh a little, his hand slides under my arse.

'I need a half.'

'Don't worry, you'll get it.'

101

I unbutton my jeans, get down on all fours on the bed, press my cheek against the stained blanket, and await the old Kabyle's cock. It's brutal when it comes, and I stifle a cry of pain; I hope he hurries up, or I'm going to scream. The old man bangs me for a little while, then comes with a groan. One eye watering from the pain, I button my jeans. The old man pulls out the plastic carrier and serves me, his movements slow. I tell him to hurry, then say that his stuff is cut too much, that he has to add a bit, so he adds a line with the point of his pocket-knife. I'm carrying my works, so I ask the old Arab if I can shoot up in his place, and he gestures towards the corner he uses as a kitchen. I shoot up the whole half. It isn't yellow, it's very light Paki, I feel it coming on as slowly as the old fucker's gestures, who is opening the door for me, leaning on his 'wife', and saying that I can come back whenever I like.

'My home is your home. One of these days, I'll fix you some couscous.'

Night is falling. My arse is dripping, I forgot to wipe up the old geezer's come, but I don't care. The Paki has calmed my pain, my legs are carrying me, my skull isn't in my guts anymore, it's on Gaîté, in the half that Ida's going to score tonight. 'I sold a bunch of stuff today,' she told me on the phone.

It isn't an escape. It's a slow death.

I've sold the chain, the cross, and the Cartier bracelet. Ida smells rotten and mouldy, her fingernails are as black as her feet. I asked Jerome for money.

'Is it to buy that rubbish?'

'No, I swear, it's to buy something to eat.'

He gave me some money, and I felt ashamed. I promised myself not to spend it all on junk, so I sacrificed a hundred francs of the five hundred to buy some food.

My doorbell started ringing like mad; I could see Alain through my peep-hole, and didn't open the door. He finally went away, leaving a nasty note on the door, calling me a bastard for borrowing money and not paying it back.

★ ★ ★

We all have the answer, tucked away in a corner of our wasted brains: an OD. I arranged to meet Ida at Montparnasse station, on the 'Grandes Lignes' side. Today's Sunday, it's four-thirty. Maybe I'll catch a glimpse of Jerome stepping into the lavatories with his suitcase in his hand. I'll hide behind a column; I won't bother him, I promise myself. It's just to see him. Ida's face is clouded by shadows as dark as her mangy fake-fur coat. We haven't had a thing in our veins since last night, and don't even have any dosh to buy Néos. This morning, we did our filters. I had a good dozen, but it still took me four fixes to get any white juice out of them. Ida just had three filters, and is sorry she hadn't saved them each time. She says she's tired of this fucking life, hustling every day to score and find dosh, what has she seen since she was fifteen years old? Fuck all. Smack. This afternoon, she had wanted to end it. She was walking along the ring road in a daze, not knowing where she was going. She came to a flyover, even put a leg over the railing, with cars streaming by below. But she lost her nerve. 'I couldn't even do that!' she says, half-crying, half-laughing. In the station, on the 'Grandes Lignes' side, she starts to bawl. She'll manage some day, she says, she'll OD, it's more radical than the motorway. What bothers her is that when you OD, you piss yourself, and she doesn't want to be found drenched in piss. I tell her that it's even worse for a bloke, that you can see the piss stain in the back of your trousers, so she should wear a skirt for her OD. I don't care if they find me covered with piss when I overdose, but I don't want to be at my place. I'll do it on the pavement late at night so nobody will bother me. But not too far away, all the same: I want to be able to see the Montparnasse tower, and imagine Jerome living behind it.

I tell Ida I'll leave her my diary, with all my fixes and the 'JTs' and 'TJs' noted in it, since it intrigues her so much. Why the notations? she wants to know. I don't know, I say, maybe I'm documenting my deterioration. Maybe the notations are screams. Before dope, I used to scream whenever I thought of Jerome, but silently. I spent days and nights silently screaming. Ida says that's never happened to her, she can't see why she'd scream in silence. I tell her that she screams every time she jabs a needle in her veins. But she doesn't get it. She says that some day she'll take a train somewhere, anywhere, she doesn't care so long as it takes her somewhere warm. We could leave together, I say, but we'll have to catch a train from the Gare de Lyon, because if you leave from Gare Montparnasse, forget about sunshine! What you get is Brittany, and I hate Brittany! From the Gare de Lyon, there are trains heading for Italy, we'll get clean there, but before we leave, we'll score a G apiece: we'll want to be cool to enjoy the scenery . . .

Ida and I have been nattering for an hour and Jerome

isn't coming. We've got to do something, get some credit, get anything. We head back to Gaîté, there isn't a soul around, not even a junkie to hit up for a bit of dosh.

We decide to pay a call on Laurence, who lives with a bloke in a little bedsitter in a Gaîté cul-de-sac. She spends all her time at the self-service launderette, washing tons of laundry, but her place is filthy and stuffy. Laurence and her boyfriend don't do much smack, just snort a couple of lines; they're more into joints. Every day, they buy a G from a black for nine hundred francs, cut it with milk sugar to make six wraps, and sell them; the difference pays for their hash.

The tiny bedsit is dripping with humidity. Laurence is lying on a mattress on the floor. Her boyfriend, whose name I don't know, is stuffing dirty laundry into big plastic carriers. We tell Laurence we're hurting, nothing since yesterday, could she help us out, even a wrap for the two of us, we'll pay her back tomorrow, she can trust us, anyway she has our phone numbers, and the other day she sold me a wrap and there was just a hundred and fifty francs' worth in it, and I gave her the kid-in-pain, she was supposed to give me fifty francs for the book and hasn't paid yet. She says she's very sorry, but she sold the last wrap half an hour ago and she has just enough money for three loads of laundry. 'It doesn't matter,' says Ida. 'Come on, let's get out of here.'

Ida seems pretty speedy. Out on the pavement I tell her we shouldn't have left so quickly.

'I'm sure if we had insisted we could have brought her round. She must have a little junk somewhere, they always snort at the end of the evening.'

'Didn't you see the night table next to the bed?'

'No, I didn't see anything. What was on it?'

'A wad of notes, for God's sake! At least three thousand francs.'

'So what?'

'You know what we're going to do? They're going to the launderette; that'll take them an hour, and when they go to the launderette they don't come straight home, they have a drink at the Liberté. All right. Did you see their door? It's just got one old lock on it, there aren't any other tenants on that floor, so we smash the door and steal the dosh.'

'Are you out of your mind? If we get busted, do you know where we'll end up?'

'It won't take us a minute! With three thousand francs we can score at least three Gs, dammit all!'

'What if they take the dosh with them?'

'Of course they won't! I'm sure of it.'

'Well, all right. You watch the landing, if there's trouble, we get out of there fast.'

I've never learned how to pick a lock, but the latch is really rotten, you can see daylight along the edge of the door. I slam my shoulder against the door and it gives, but I feel the noise I made must have roused the whole building. I grab the wad from the little night table next to the mattress.

'You got the money?'

'Yes.'

'How much is there?'

'Christ! You think I had the time to count it? Come on, let's scarper, we better not score around here tonight.'

We catch a cab on avenue du Maine and head for

106

Réaumur-Sébastopol. I count the notes: two thousand seven hundred francs. 'Bloody marvellous!' screams Ida who isn't crying anymore, who doesn't feel like catching a train, who's kissing me on the cheek and saying that everything's coming up roses.

★ ★ ★

I'm in an urban landscape, standing on an iron walkway, the sky is blue along the horizon. My eye moves from the blue horizon up into the sky, where the blue fades into grey, then black. Towers loom against the black background. The sun can't be seen, but it's glittering on the glass and steel of the towers. There's water at the foot of the towers, lakes, I think; the water is a more intense blue than the horizon. I cross other walkways, climb some spiral stairs, reach an open space, a courtyard at the level of the next-to-the-last-storey of the tallest tower. There is a swimming pool in the middle of the courtyard, with blue sky in the open space above it. I look through a window of the next-to-the-last-storey, see a silhouette behind the panes, can't make it out very well but suppose it's Paris-Tokyo. He opens the window and spreads sheets, a bolster, pillows and a blanket on the sill; Jerome hasn't come. I sit down at the edge of the pool and wait for Jerome. I will stay as long as I have to, but I'm determined to see him. The sky, the open space, the towers, and the walkways all vanish. I was naked all the way through the dream, passing people who didn't notice my nakedness. I'm often naked in my dreams. It's seven a.m. This is the second time I've dreamed this and it makes me feel uneasy. I need a fix. Constipation be damned.

★ ★ ★

The manuscript is ninety-eight pages long. A box of Néons has become a permanent fixture on the white plywood table. I hand the pages over to the man with the dead arm and he gives me a cheque. Gs are eight hundred francs; I'm mentally dividing the amount of the cheque by eight hundred.

Ida was at my place as Pierre was shooting up. I gave him some cotton-wool to wipe up the blood. He crouched down next to a low black plastic table. When I asked him what he was doing bent down like that, he answered that he was tying his shoelaces. After he left, I looked at the low table: my cigarette case was missing. And Pierre had been wearing boots without laces. We took off after him, but he was too far away, and running too fast. Ida and I combed Saint-Germain and Montparnasse searching for the filthy shit, to beat the crap out of him, but we didn't find him.

I was just waking up from a dreamless sleep when my cock came. I pushed down the sheets and saw the sperm flowing from my limp cock. A transparent whitish trickle, like juice. Corpse juice.

'We'll have smack tonight, Ida, lots of smack, and it won't cost us a penny.'

'On tick?'

'Nope. I've got a plan. I'll tell you about it.'

I was sitting on the edge of the bed next to the old Arab. He bared his gold teeth, squeezed my thigh, I unbuttoned my jeans and laid my cheek on the stained blanket. I clenched my teeth and fists as the old Kabyle stuck his cock up my arse. I asked him for a cloth to wipe myself. He was talking about couscous again as he set the plastic carrier on the table. Then I moved very fast: I shoved the old man, who fell between the bed and the table, grabbed the carrier, made for the door and turned the lock. The old bloke started shouting in Arabic, the other Arabs in the squatters' building would show up at any minute. I clattered down the stairs. As I ran down the street I turned around and saw two Arabs coming out of the place, but I had a good lead. I ran all the way to Montparnasse without stopping and collapsed at the foot of a building, my lungs about to burst. Breathing deeply, I got my wind back and started laughing and crying with joy, hugging the parcel to my chest.

'Bloody marvellous! There must be at least ten Gs here! Where did you get it?'

'I nicked it from an old Arab on rue Daguerre! You know what we're going to do? We'll take two Gs apiece, and sell the rest.'

'That's brilliant! But why don't we cut it with milk sugar?'

'It's already been cut to death.'

'Yes, but instead of making twenty wraps, we'll have thirty.'

'All right.'

We shot up a good half wrap, bought milk sugar, cut up paper into little pieces, and made thirty wraps which we sold in Réaumur-Sébastopol. I had to avoid Gaîté for a few days, so I spent them glued in front of my Olympia from nine in the morning to five in the evening without a break.

Jerome gave me some money. I rang up my brother and told him I owed a bloke some dosh, five hundred francs, and he gave them to me. Then I ran into Marc and got three hundred out of him.

Sitting at the Liberté, Ida and I had to wait for a waiter for a long time. I gestured to him and he came over, but said he didn't want to serve us. When I asked why, he said he wasn't serving addicts anymore. I started shouting, but Ida motioned for me to be quiet. So we got up and went to another café, one that does serve addicts.

We're in a deserted street in Bagneux, at one of Ida's connections. We had arranged to meet a black bloke at I a.m., but when he came by, he said there was a hold up, that he'd get the smack in two hours, that we had to wait. By now, it's three o'clock, and we aren't talking; we're cold and hurting too much. At three-thirty, the black serves us two wraps of brown. From her bag, Ida pulls out the spikes, a lemon and a spoon, but we don't have any water. There isn't a single bar open, and the gutters are dry. I can't last another minute.

'I'm going to piss in my spike. We don't have any choice.'

'Are you out of your mind? You aren't going to stick piss in your veins?'

'Listen, with all the shit we shoot up, a little piss isn't going to kill us.'

In a building entrance, I pull the plunger out of my spike and piss into the syringe.

'What the hell, you're right,' says Ida, who lifts her skirt, pulls down her knickers, and squats.

'Be careful. Don't shit in your spike.'

'Don't make me laugh, goddamn it! You think it's easy for a woman to piss into a syringe?'

The mixture had an odd smell. We walk back up to Montparnasse. It's 4 a.m., Jerome must be sleeping next to Paris-Tokyo. In a few hours, he'll be hearing the shouts of the children.

Gaîté has been raided. The filth sealed off the neighbourhood, fanned out into the Liberté, nailed Rashid and his stash bags, Saadi, Ciel, and a few other junkies. All this happened while Ida and I were shooting up our piss at Bagneux, with everything coming up roses.

The cops searched Saadi's place and found two scales and some powder. They tore Rashid apart down at the narcotics division. He was hurting and wanted to get the hell out of that rat-hole. Ciel says they beat him so badly you could hardly recognize him. Ciel herself spent two weeks in hospital, including three days in a coma caused by going cold turkey behind bars, before she was released. Rashid's in the nick, but the cops have turned Saadi loose. Did he cut a deal with them? Nobody knows. Battered from going cold turkey, Ciel says she's had it with smack; maybe a snort from time to time, but no more shooting up. The Gaîté connection is dead.

Ida has found another connection, a black who deals out of Nadège's place. Nadège snorts smack, and I turned her on one night when she was hurting. I gave her a line from a wrap I scored from an Arab at the Pernety métro, and she snorted it in her car while she was double-parked on rue Raymond-Losserand. Nadège is a tall, good-looking blonde who wears a pink fake-fur coat. She works as a bookkeeper in a big insurance agency and pays for her lines, her Portuguese

111

husband Gilberto's daily fix, food for Linda, their three-
year-old, and the rent on a dusty, messy three-room
flat on rue Maison-Dieu. I'm sitting there next to Ida,
waiting for Prosper, the black dealer, to show up. Gilberto is tall and very thin, he's drinking wine straight
from the bottle; Linda, a tiny girl as dark as her father,
clings to our legs. We're silent, our nerves on edge.

'What does your black look like, Ida?'

'You don't know him, he's a street-corner connection. You'll see, he has a face that belongs on the
Muppet Show!'

Two Portuguese blokes show up to be served, then
a third. There isn't any room left on the sofa-bed,
the Portuguese are sitting on the linoleum with Linda
climbing all over them. Then Muppet Show comes in.
He's fat, with very dark skin. The hood of his sweatshirt pulled right down to his watery, bulging eyes. A
face from hell. 'Hey Ida, are those his nostrils or a pair
of Ray-Bans?'

He slowly takes off his sweatshirt, removes one sweater, two sweaters, three. He's a lot less fat now and still
has two or three sweaters on and a shirt.

'Come on, Prosper, move it!'

'God, you're a pain. You done with the strip-tease
yet?'

'We've been waiting two hours for you.'

'Yes . . . All right, you blokes . . . yeah,' he says,
barely above a mumble. Muppet Show explains that
the cops busted him last night and searched him at
headquarters, but got fed up with all the clothes and
told him to clear off. He pulls down his first pair of
jogging trousers, then a second, slips a hand between
the third and the fourth and pulls out a parcel wrapped

in clear plastic. Muppet Show serves us and we start to talk and smile again. Ida and I shoot up in the kitchen, the others in the kitchen-living room. Gilberto slaps Linda. 'Jesus Christ, don't touch my spike!' he says. 'Nadège! Can't you get this kid to sleep? Look at the time!'

'Hey, do you mind if I do my line?'

Muppet Show changes hotels every night. When he doesn't show up at rue Maison-Dieu on time, Ida and I make the rounds of all the Arab-run no-star hotels from Denfert-Rochereau to Alésia and from Raymond-Losserand to avenue René-Coty. We never find him, so we come back to rue Maison-Dieu and wait. He shows up at midnight, one, or two in the morning, completely loaded on the heroin cigarettes he smokes from morning till night.

'When Nadège got pregnant,' says Ida, 'they decided to kick the habit. They'd gone clean, they were cool, but when they got the news, it knocked them for six, so they went back to smack. Nadège wanted to get an abortion, but Gilberto didn't want her to. The result: the kid's HIV-positive.'

* * *

'Every week you say it, and you never go through with it.'

'Yes, but this time I'm really quitting. I won't take anything tomorrow, and anyway I don't have any dosh, so the time's right.'

Next morning, I swallow twenty Néos, then finish the other box that afternoon with two Seresta 50s. That night, I have dinner at a mate's house, the two of use drink three litres of wine. By midnight, I'm pounding

113

on the door of the rue Maison–Dieu flat. Muppet Show has already been there and gone. So has Ida, who scored a half, waited to turn me on and then took off. I tell Gilberto that he has to help me out, I don't have a penny. Just a little fix, some filter juice. 'You blokes are a pain in the arse,' he says. 'This isn't the Salvation Army. When I'm hurting, I don't bother anybody.' I start to cry. 'Christ, I turned Nadège on once,' I say. 'You're a fucker, you could at least help me out.' He heaves a sigh, Nadège nods yes, and he says, 'All right, but just a sample. Hand me your spoon.'

'I don't have my works with me.'

'Jesus, you're a pain!'

There's a brown crust in his spoon. One day, when Nadège wanted to clean the spoon, she got a slap across the face. Gilberto can be violent when he's hurting. With a knife, he scrapes a sample of Paki on to the crust.

'I don't have my spike.'

'Is that so? Don't you know you aren't supposed to borrow somebody else's spike? What will I have to shoot up with tomorrow?'

'You can just rinse it with bleach.'

I ask him to fix me, I'm too fucked up to find my vein, I'm shaking. Gilberto fixes me. He's a really nice bloke, I tell him, a real mate, I won't forget this. I stumble out of the place. I can't stomach the geezer, he gives me the creeps, he's no mate of mine.

I collapse on the steps of the wooden ladder. The phone rings: it's Ida. She's talking, but I can't hear what she's saying. I'm dreaming with my eyes open. In my dream, someone's talking to me, and I'm answering aloud. From time to time I shake my head and move my body a little to remind myself that Ida's on the line. 'What the hell are you talking about?' I hear her say. 'Jesus, you're too far gone!' I hang up and collapse on the wooden steps fully dressed. In the morning, my body's stiff and sore, and there's a wet stain between my legs.

Nadège and Gilberto are fed up with all the people trooping through their place and the spikes lying around the kitchen. It isn't good for Linda, who plays with the syringes and ought to be put to bed early, not at one in the morning. I give Muppet Show my address so he can come by and serve me. His woman is in gaol for purse-snatching, she was the one who used to deal, so he deals to send her dosh. She'll be out soon, but he doesn't feel safe because his papers aren't in order. All he has is a Zairian ID card he bought for seven hundred francs from an African in Goutte-d'Or. Muppet Show claims he's a political refugee and wants to ask for asylum, but doesn't know how to write French. Ida and I don't believe a word of it, but it's a good way to get some credit. I tell him I'll take care of his papers, but I haven't a penny tonight and I'm hurting, and so is Ida. It would be nice if he'd let us cop on tick. He can't, he says, his woman would find out, even in prison she knows everything, and she's hard to handle.

'Jesus, what a loser you are! You don't mind letting me help you with your papers but then you leave us hurting.'

He serves us a half with the point of his knife, then abruptly asks Ida if she'll sleep with him.

'Listen, Prosper, you're a good mate and I like you, but I don't feel like sleeping with you. And there's your woman.'

115

'All right, it doesn't matter. But think about it.'

His watery eyes are smiling, he's fondling Ida's bottom the way you stroke a dog's back.

I draft a letter for Muppet Show in which he declares that when he was a student in Kinshasa he distributed leaflets on campus that the authorities judged subversive. I go on to detail his arrest and torture, his escape from the country thanks to a little money given him by his parents, who run a small business in the capital, his condemnation to death *in absentia*, his request for political asylum. I also draw up a certificate of residence stating that Muppet Show has been living at my place for a few months. The cost is a half-wrap of Paki he'll give me tomorrow, Sunday, in a squatter's building in rue de Texel. He's been living there for the last three days with a cousin he ran into by chance in Barbès.

I climb the building's two flights of stairs and give my name through the door. A tall, very skinny black lets me in and leads the way through a room cluttered with cardboard boxes, suitcases and old broken furniture, to another room that has bricked-up windows and walls covered with posters of various soccer teams. The tall black lies down on a mattress on the floor and curls up in some faded blankets. There's a telly on a low chest of drawers, and another on the floor. The black cousin's mattress lies at the foot of a bed, and lying in the bed next to Muppet Show is Ida. She pretends to be surprised to see me in this filthy shit-hole at noon on a Sunday. Embarrassed, she sits up on the edge of the bed, takes her works from a night table, and prepares a fix. Muppet Show gets up; he's naked, and I notice he's almost skinny. He serves me my half, and I leave.

'See you.'

116

There's a stench in my nostrils, a stench of filth and Ida. The sky is pure blue, it'll be spring soon, the weather over the white house must be fine. I don't give a damn about the seasons.

'Nothing happened with Prosper, you know.'

'Look, Ida, whatever you want to do with your arse is your business.'

'Nothing happened, I tell you! He wanted to touch me and I told him to get lost. I just slept there, that's all. I'd never fuck for dope.'

'All right, you just slept there. I believe you.'

There's a lump inside her right elbow, with a black hole in the centre. I squeeze it, and pus flows out. Left arm: same lump, same black hole, more pus. I tell Ida she must find another place for her fix; lower down, towards her wrist. She doesn't want to, no other tracks, you never know, what if a customer noticed, or the cops, or her lover boss? He already suspects something, one day she's soaring, one day she's speedy . . . She jabs the needle in with a little cry, probes, searching for the vein, starts to sweat. I shout at her, saying that it shouldn't take forever to do a hit, that I need her spike, *my* spike.

Muppet Show's Paki is more and more cut, he's more and more loaded, and Ida hurts less and less. He comes by one night with his face battered, one eye closed, his lip split; a wrangle with another black dealer. His woman is out of prison and Muppet Show got busted between two deliveries. This time the cops took the time to undress him.

A phone call from Séverine: I got her into deep shit with that business with the old Kabyle, but she straightened it out. She says she just made a few buys.

I'm carrying two books I bought; one is *Snow White*, the other has a brown cover. I sell the brown one by weight, seven hundred francs a gram, a thousand for *Snow White*.

I don't have a penny but I tell her to stop by, I'll try to twist her arm.

Séverine says she can't give me credit, but she needs clothes for the bloke she lives with in a squatters' building in Saint-Michel. If I can give her some clothes that aren't too worn she'll see what she can do. I open my wardrobe and pile up the clothes I plan to swap for a wrap of Paki that's been cut to death.

Ciel is at Laurence's. The swelling in her face has gone down and there are needle tracks along her jugular. She says a girl is dealing for Saadi, but not at Gaîté. She deals at Palais-Royal after she's finished work. We know her, she's a Portuguese bint with glasses, a twisted mouth, faded blonde hair and a big arse; she came to my place a couple of times with some Portuguese blokes who didn't have a place to shoot up. We call her Maria the Stinkpot, because she farts after she shoots up; she can't help it, smack just destroys her guts. One night, my neighbour, a bitch who lets an old fuck screw her while she plays opera music, came out when Maria was on the landing. She had been farting and it smelled bad. We were listening behind the door, and when Stinkpot wanted to come in we locked her out, laughing like lunatics. It had been months since I'd laughed like that. I let her in, and she swore at us, calling us a bunch of

118

shitty addicts. But then she cut one last fart in the middle of her Portuguese harangue, and we creased up laughing, so she slammed the door and left.

Three Portuguese are waiting on a bench at Palais-Royal. Yesterday, Ida loaned Stinkpot a gold ring that belonged to her grandmother, for a wrap. She was supposed to buy the ring back today, but doesn't have any dosh; I owe Stinkpot fifty francs and I don't have any money either. Maria's speedy when she shows up, and shouts for us to wait in that café over there, not in the street. She serves the three Portuguese. Ida tries to bring her round, says we'll have dosh tomorrow, it's a promise, but she has to have the ring back. I offer her my diamond earring, it's a tenth of a carat, but Stinkpot says she doesn't want jewellery, she wants cash. Ida says she's had it with this Portuguese bitch who's always speedy. She turned her on a couple of times and this is the thanks she gets. Ida says she's going to pull a dirty trick on her. She suggests we rob her.

'Nobody's on the streets at this hour, and she always carries the shit in her bag.'

'We can't rip her off. She'd recognize us, and you can imagine what hassles we'd have with Saadi.'

'We've got to find someone to do it. But not an addict.'

'I don't know a soul.'

'I'll find someone. At Créteil there are lots of kids who'd jump at the chance.'

Ida finds a fifteen-year-old black kid in trainers with a Walkman. She tells him the woman will be walking along rue Saint-Honoré and that he should grab her bag when she reaches rue des Pyramides. We'll be waiting for him at the corner of avenue de l'Opéra and rue des Petits-Champs. We point out Stinkpot to him, and he follows her. As we stroll up avenue de l'Opéra, Ida says she's sure it will work.

The black kid calmly walks up to us with a bulge under his jacket, laughing. He says he yanked so hard the woman fell down screaming. We search the bag: five wraps, some money, the ring. We take the wraps and the ring, and give the kid the bag and the dosh. Saadi isn't going to like this one bit.

Séverine's on the phone: it's all set, they've got everything they need, smack and a place to live on rue du Faubourg-Saint-Jacques near the Port-Royal métro. They'll be serving from half past noon on.

Her boyfriend's name is Kader, he's Algerian. He has curly hair, a broken nose, a slim muscular body, and a gold right eye-tooth. The flat is tiny, two rooms on the ground floor facing a courtyard, with a toilet out on the landing. They're lying down. Without getting up, Kader serves me a wrap which I shoot up in the corner kitchen. No rush, no nothing.

'Shit, your smack's milk sugar!'

'No, it isn't. I swear we don't cut it, do we, Kader?'

I bring a wrap back to Ida, who says it's garbage. We go looking for another connection.

I'm on the platform of the Réaumur-Sébastopol métro, Porte de Clignancourt side. There are blacks everywhere, sitting and standing around. 'You looking for something?' 'You want some stuff?' 'Hi, man, what are you looking for?' I want heroin, I say. The black says he has some Paki that'll really blow my head off. He pulls out a parcel of powder, a pocket-knife, and a piece of paper right there on the platform, and serves me a half in front of the people getting on and off the train. They don't look surprised.

On the plywood table, I heat the powder in the spoon. It clots. There's no way to draw the junk up into the spike. I heat the rest of the half with spirits and lemon juice. More clots. The fucking black sold me plaster! Four hundred francs worth of brown plaster! Ida comes in with a big smile under her black eyes. I tell her I've been taken for four hundred francs. She thinks I'm kidding, so I show her the spoon with the cold clots. She collapses on to a chair, says she closed the shop up early to get here sooner, that she was riding the métro thinking of the half I had waiting for her. Ida is crying; in the last few minutes, she's aged twenty years. There's only one possibility left: Séverine and Kader. With a little luck we'll find them at Saint-Jacques and bring them round. I think Kader likes me.

We stick our wasted bodies in a bus for Port-Royal.

I tell Kader about Réaumur, tell him we can't hold out, that we'll have money tomorrow, but he has to give us credit for tonight. He says he usually doesn't give tick but he'll see what he can do, just this once. He tells Séverine to pull out the notebook. She opens a schoolboy notebook with a blue cover and writes our names on the first page, with '200' next to them. We thank Kader, tell him how great he is, you don't find sellers like him. We do our fix in the kitchen, Séverine offers us tea, we accept. The smack doesn't seem as cut as last time, it warms us better.

There's a regular parade through the two-room flat: a black with his kid, a rock musician, some blokes I don't know who leave after shooting up. A joint is passed around. Kader doesn't use smack, but he smokes good hash from a fat black lump shaped like a bar of soap. If we don't find him at home in the evening, he says, someone's dealing for him over by Port-Royal, at the Crystal café. 'It's Joao,' says Séverine, 'the Portuguese bloke who used to sell for Saadi at Gaîté.' Tomorrow morning, I'll shoot up my filters and set out to find dosh to score at twelve-thirty. I arrange to meet Ida tomorrow at rue du Faubourg-Saint-Jacques.

★ ★ ★

Jerome's birthday will be in a few days, at the white house, during the Easter holiday. He'll be forty-six. I manage to scrape together some money to buy and post him two old engravings. 'POJ' on 30 March. There are nine 'JTs' during the Easter break. I'm floundering in my manuscript. Tomorrow I'll get clean. Tomorrow, I fail.

★ ★ ★

In spite of his daily half-wrap, Joao's as speedy as ever, and he still has that habit of hawking and spitting every couple of minutes. He says that Claudine's away in the country getting clean, that he isn't selling at the Crystal, but a little further on, in rue Henri-Barbusse. We enter a building, take a lift down to the third level underground. We cross a car park and reach the cellars. One of them has a yellow mattress on the floor, two wooden crates for tables, with a bottle of water, an ashtray, lemon juice, and a candle: the lights are always going out. Joao's woman serves the customers, talking softly, telling them to shut up and not to piss on the cellar doors. A bloke asks someone to tie him off, a woman's looking for a spike, another one wants to be turned on. Pale faces in the half-light. Miniel is there, the Yugoslav who snatches handbags to pay for his fixes. We score the last wrap.

We don't have our works, so I ask for a syringe. Joao offers me his. I ask him if he's HIV-positive and he answers 'No' just as the lights go out. I crouch down, Ida ties me off, I search my hand for a vein that isn't too messed up. I dig it in, rinse the spike and hand it to her. It's midnight. Joao says he has arranged to see Kader in two hours, who has gone to Stalingrad to make a buy. Ida lies down on the yellow mattress to wait for the next delivery. She curls up facing the wall and I stretch out behind her, my body against hers. In the stench of the cellars, I can't smell her. Jerome and I were naked on the navy-blue quilt, I had taken him in my arms, silently kissed his face, my mouth sound-less on his skin. He had closed his eyes, sighed. He was feeling good. 'It must be nice to sleep in your arms,' he murmured. With just a half-wrap apiece, we won't last two hours.

Couscous over at Kader and Séverine's, mint tea, hash from a pipe in a glass of water, smoked hubble-bubble style. A fix with dessert. Kader says he's been in France for six years, incognito, without a residence permit. He wants to get his papers in order, but doesn't know how, and neither does Séverine. He asks if I can take care of it. You can count on me, I answer. The credit in the schoolboy notebook is growing: fifteen hundred francs for me, eight hundred for Ida. We're mates, Kader says. He calls me his brother.

We carefully checked the place out. The kitchen opens

on to a sort of courtyard two yards square, no shutters
on the window, and nothing across the way. We figured
there might be a little junk at Kader's – Séverine's
powder. I had noticed that when she gets up at half
past twelve, she snorts a line from a parcel of smack
that's separate from the one for the customers: *her*
smack, uncut. I wrap my jacket around my hand and
break the window-pane under the latch. Ida's in the
hallway standing guard while I search the flat, turning
over the bed, moving the furniture. But there's no
smack, just a chipped block of hash.

I tell Kader that when I got here yesterday I saw a
bloke running down the hallway, a very speedy Arab.

'What did he look like?'

'Tall and thin, with very curly black hair.'

'Was he wearing a leather jacket?'

'Er, yeah, a black jacket . . . leather.'

'Did he have a scar on his cheek?'

'You know, it was night-time, I didn't get a good
look at his face. Ida, did you notice if the bloke had a
scar on his face?'

Ida pretends to think.

'Frankly, I couldn't say, he rushed right past me.'

Kader tells Séverine that he knows the bloke, and
he'll skin the sod alive for breaking into his flat.

'What we ought to do,' says Ida, 'is deal. We could
suggest it to Kader. He doesn't have any customers at
Montparnasse and we could find him a million of them.'

I tell Ida that it's a good idea, but we shouldn't do it
on the street. We have to deal here, at my place, it's
cooler and a connection in a flat isn't as dangerous. I
put it to Kader, who says he's willing, it just so happens

he wants to talk to me about it. 'Coincidences are funny, brother.' Kader phones his customers and tells them that from now on he'll serve them at my flat. They have to ring up first, and I'll say, 'Kader will be coming at such-and-such a time,' and they'll drop by then. Ida's pissed off, and so am I. This wasn't what we were hoping for, we wanted Kader to give us the smack, and pay us in smack.

I start taking calls. 'Yes, Kader will be here in an hour.' 'No, it'll be another two hours.' 'I don't know, he hasn't rung up yet.' The junkies sit or lie around on the carpet, shaking, silent or talkative, waiting for Kader. I don't mind their shooting up here but they have to turn me on from time to time, a sample apiece.

One evening Kader doesn't come – some hold up over by Stalingrad – and it's panic time on the carpet, with a woman handing out Equanyl tablets that she bought for ten francs apiece from a black at les Halles. Kader gives me uncut wraps. In the schoolboy notebook with the blue cover, '7000' has been written next to my name; '1 G' appears on every page of my diary.

★ ★ ★

The last lines of the manuscript: one evening, the handsome drunk dies after getting a terrific punch in the face, not far from the La Rochelle towers, in front of the two kids born of the kid-in-pain's mother's torn vagina. It ends on the image of that bloody evening, which the older of the two kids will remember. The other won't; he was sleeping, perhaps dreaming.

I mix everything up, spread the sheets out on the carpet. A puzzle. I shuffle and stack the pages, this chapter comes after that one, this one before that. There

125

are bloodstains on some of the pages I've run through the Olympia. I make corrections, cut and paste, number the pages of a story that will go up in injected powder. I give the mother, the drunk and the two kids to the man with the dead arm in exchange for a cheque. Then I write to a foundation that helps needy writers, asking for money.

'Hey man, what have you been up to?'

It was Frank; I'd forgotten all about him and his donkey dick. On the phone he says that he's pretty much kicked the habit, that he's living with a psychiatric nurse in a bedsitter by the Porte des Lilas. When he does the occasional fix, his girlfriend gives him hell. Smack isn't her thing, and she says she'll ditch him if he doesn't stop messing around. But he's hooked on her, and he fucks her so much, some nights she shouts, 'More, more!' and others 'Stop, I can't take it anymore.' He says he's been doing a little temp work, but isn't working right now, doesn't have any dosh but would really like to score today, it would be cool if I'd turn him on, shit, I'd be a real prince.

His cheeks are full, you can't see the bones on his face anymore. He says he's gained twenty pounds, is in terrific shape, and his cock's hard as a rock. He can hardly piss, he says; it isn't easy when you've got a hard-on. I share my half with him.

Frank phones often and never has any money, but I turn him on when he drops by. He's a world-class parasite, but he makes me smile, so I don't mind. And he still talks a mile a minute. He says that when he was a kid he used to feel really self-conscious because of his weight: he weighed two hundred and ninety pounds until he was twenty, and you could hardly see his eyes; his face looked like somebody's arse. Doing junk melted him down fast, now he weighs a hundred and fifty-five girls are mad about him, he fucks like mad, it isn't true that kids who are born fat have little cocks.

'Here, let me show you, you're queer, you can tell me, you must have seen lots of cocks. Have a look. My cock isn't small, is it?'

'No, of course not, it's normal.'

'What about my balls? A little on the small side, don't you think?'

'Jesus, what a pain you are! Your balls are normal too!'

One day Ida came by while Frank was shooting up. Her eyes looked loaded, so I didn't turn her on.

'Why should I turn you on, you're completely stoned. Do you ever turn me on? You never have any dosh! How did you get loaded, anyway?'

'Hey, what's with you? I haven't had anything since this morning!'

'Cut the bullshit. I asked Kader, and he told me you score a half every day, so don't treat me like an idiot!'

'What a sod that Kader is. A right Arab wog!'

'Where do you get your money? Prosper's out of the nick and he's screwing you, is that it?'

'You're a real arsehole, you know that?'

'You're right, you bitch, we're all arseholes!'

She left, calling me a queer, said I could take Jerome and go fuck myself, and slammed the door. I yanked it open again; Ida was at the end of the hallway.

128

'And don't bother showing up here anymore! Even if you're hurting, you can go screw yourself!'

'I'd rather die than ever ask you for a line, creep!'

This time, I was the one who slammed the door. I was shaking. I shot up the rest of the smack, telling myself that she could peg out at my feet and I wouldn't give a good goddamn, that I'd wipe my arse with her, the bitch!

Séverine and Kader got thrown out of their place; the landlady got tired of all the comings and goings and didn't like Arabs who don't work. You need salary records to land a flat, but I tell Kader I'll do what I can. I visit the man who didn't commit suicide in his suburban chartered accountant's office: green plants, fake-marble Greek statues, plastic furniture, computers, and a young, male staff. I ask him for three fake pay stubs showing a high salary for me. Then I get a shop to make up a rubber stamp with the name and address of a phoney company, buy a pay book, and fill out three stubs in Séverine's name. We visit some estate agents and locate a two-room place on boulevard de Grenelle. I pay the agent the first and last month's rent with a wad of thousand-franc notes that Kader gave me.

The cheque for the mother's story comes but I don't mention it to Kader; I'm moving in two weeks and need the money for my first days at a hotel. Thanks to the fake pay stubs and the story, '2 Gs' appears on every page of my diary. A fix at eight o'clock, a fix at ten, a fix at noon; a fix every two hours. I spend my days with my brother Kader and his woman Séverine, then climb into their red car at night and accompany them as they deal. We stop at Port-Royal to serve Joao; I

wait in the car. We head for Denfert–Rochereau; Kader
serves two Gs to a waiting woman who is pushing her
kid in a pram, and a G to a very tall blond bloke. We
go to a run-down tenement in Châtillon; Kader serves
three Gs to a junkie who cuts the smack in half with
milk sugar and resells it. Then we go to place d'Italie
and Kader serves a bloke waiting in a grey car. Along
the way we stop at a bar, where I do a fix, and I do
another fix in the bloke at Châtillon's bathroom.

'Can you serve me a half, Kader?'
 'Are you joking? I've served you nearly three Gs
already.'
 'You must be out of your mind. You served me a G
and a half, tops!'
 'Jesus, can't you remember?'
 'No, not really. My memory's shot.'

★ ★ ★

'Here, I'm giving you my stereo set,' I tell Kader.
 'Why me?'
 'I have too much stuff to move. You're my mate, I'd
rather give it to you.'
 He thanks me, says he's cutting my outstanding
balance to show his appreciation for the stereo.
 'You owe me seven thousand five. Let's say that you
owe me only . . . three thousand five, without counting
the G today.'
 'That's really nice of you, Kader. But you know, I
didn't give you the stereo for credit.'
 He knows, he says, and smiles with his gold eye-
tooth.

I don't bother writing the Gs in my diary anymore. Just the 'JTs' and the 'TJs'.

★   ★   ★

Kader hasn't opened his mouth, hasn't said a word all day except, 'Get in the car, in the back.' We don't stop at Port-Royal, or Denfert-Rochereau, or Châtillon, or place d'Italie; we're heading straight for Barbès. I ask him to stop at a bar, it's been two hours since my last fix. 'Wait a bit,' Kader answers dryly. He double-parks on boulevard Barbès, and a woman climbs in and sits down without saying a word. I can't see her face, just her very long black hair. Kader roars off. He's driving like a maniac, the girl asks where we're going, her tone begging, on the verge of tears. Kader doesn't answer. We're outside Paris now, in the northern suburbs. 'We're just out for a ride,' says Kader with a smile. I tell Séverine I've got to have my fix. She puts a finger to her lips and says, 'Shhh.' The night is as black as Kader's staring eyes in the rear-view mirror.

We stop in a spooky neighbourhood, at a dimly-lit vacant lot strewn with jumbled blocks of cement; it looks like an abandoned construction site. Kader switches off the engine. 'Now tell me what happened.' The girl starts to cry, asks for a line. 'Later,' Kader answers coldly. The girl says it's the truth, that she was making up the wraps and the five Gs fell on the carpet, and it's a deep-pile carpet and she wasn't able to salvage the powder, it's true, Kader has to believe her. She's watching Kader as she talks, I can see her face in profile now, her hooked nose and high cheekbones, her smeared mascara. Then I see something gleaming at the junkie's throat: Kader's knife. He's turned his head and

131

is looking at her, says not to take him for a fool, the carpet trick's an old one, it's been tried before. The weeping girl hiccoughs, wipes the snot dribbling from her nose with the back of her hand. Why doesn't he just slit her throat, or else stop this routine, anything so long as he serves me, things are breaking loose in my skull, I feel the pain starting to race through my guts. Now the girl's begging: 'I swear it's true, Kader, I swear on the head of my child. I'll be careful next time.' She says she'll pay him back, she swears again.

The knife disappears. Kader says he believes her this once, but that she has to be very careful in the future. 'All right, it's all over, calm down,' he says, stroking the junkie's cheek. 'See, it all works out. We'll work out the dosh too.' He turns around to Séverine and tells her to serve us a good wrap, 'It's a present from me.' The girl sniffles. 'Thanks Kader, you're really nice.' Smiling, Kader passes me a bottle of mineral water. I get out, and the girl and I shoot up on a block of cement, I in my hand, she in the jugular, looking for her vein in a small hand-mirror she's taken from her bag. We're talking and laughing now, Kader has put on a cassette of Arab music, he asks the junkie how her kid is doing. We're driving back to Barbès. Kader's eye-tooth gleams in the rear-view mirror.

★   ★   ★

A clean flat in a white building in the fourteenth *arrondissement*. Séverine, Kader and a girl are sitting on the living-room sofa. I ask if I can fix there, the girl says, 'Yes, there's some cotton-wool on the kitchen table and vinegar in the fridge.' I prepare my works on the

132

formica table while listening to the girl discuss credit with Kader.

'You owe me eight hundred, that's too much, I can't trust you anymore.'

'But I'm getting paid tomorrow. I'll pay you back tomorrow, I swear.'

'What if all my customers asked for credit? What would I have to buy smack with?'

'Come on, it's no problem for you, if you want to give somebody smack on tick, you can do it.'

'You addicts are a laugh! You think it's easy?'

'What about your mate in the kitchen, can't he turn me on?'

The mate digs the needle into his hand, pulls the plunger to watch the blood rise in the spike to be sure it's in the vein, then hears a whimper to his right, near the window. He turns his head and sees a baby sitting on a chair with a transparent plastic potty under its arse. The baby is banging on the chair's tray with a little silver spoon. It smiles, showing two tiny white teeth in its upper jaw. Not stumps yet. It's cooing and smiling, babbling to the mate pushing the plunger. The mate says, 'Hello there! This won't take a minute.' He rinses his spike in the sink next to the jars of Blédina baby food, and asks Kader to give the kid's mother a sample.

* * *

Séverine and Kader have moved out without paying the rent or leaving a forwarding address. So have I. I packed whatever I hadn't sold to buy dope into cardboard boxes and stored them in a room at the school for handicapped kids. Jerome asked if I wanted some money, I said yes, and he gave me six hundred francs.

133

I stowed my suitcase, my syringe, and my G in a hotel on rue de l'Arrivée. I'll have to find something else tomorrow, I can't afford three hundred and fifty francs a night.

I have a little money left, enough to score my two to three daily Gs for a few days.

Kader's brother and cousin have arrived from Algeria. The brother is a customs agent at the airport, the cousin's a cop, also at the airport. Kader reminds me that I owe him money.

'Do you know how much you owe me?'

'Not really. About four thousand, isn't it?'

'What, are you joking? You owe me seven thousand five.'

'Cut the bullshit. I have some dosh now.'

'Séverine, the notebook! Look: one G on Tuesday, plus a half, plus a G, plus . . .'

'Shit! I didn't realize I owed you so much.'

'All right. I'll cross out the first Gs. There. Let's say you only owe me . . . five thousand.'

'Bloody hell, that's nice of you. Thanks, Kader, you're a real mate.'

'Don't mention it. You aren't like the other addicts. There's a favour I may want to ask you sometime, but there's no hurry. We'll talk about it some other time, brother.'

I telephone Sylvain, a bloke who once wrote to me to say how much he'd liked the kid-in-pain book. We had met three times, the first time he bought a small sketch on felt for two hundred francs. It came at just the right time, I was hurting. He drove me over to rue Maison-

Dieu and I was able to score a wrap at Gilberto and Nadège's. On the phone, I ask Sylvain if he can put me up for a few days. No problem, he answers.

Tuesday, 7 June. I take a cab to the twentieth *arrondissement*, near the Pelleport métro station, and move in with Sylvain, with my bag, my spike and my powder.

★ ★ ★

Sylvain is a slim thirty-year-old with straight black hair and a silver ring in his ear. Sitting on the black sofa in his big living room with its bare white walls, he tells me his own kid-in-pain story. He describes his middle-class childhood, the Catholic boarding school, the provincial college he attended to become an engineer, just like Dad. Mum didn't work, but she'd done a bit of everything: radio announcer, model, a bunch of other things. The kid was suffocating between Mum-and-Dad and the college, so he ran away, hopped a plane for Puerto Rico. In San Juan he discovered men's cocks in a wealthy solicitor's semi-detached: there were seven young blokes, and they buggered the twenty-year-old one after another. The kid liked it. Elsewhere, he also discovered women, and screwed them savagely. Bumfucks in Cairo, Barcelona, Tunis, Tangier, life with all the stops pulled out. Sylvain talks about Jim Morisson, the Doors, Piaf, Argentine tango. He talks about American films, Burroughs, Genet, cocaine. He talks about fucking, but not about love: Sylvain takes, but he doesn't give. I tell him about Jerome and dreaming the great love for so long, the writing offered, the dream's failure, the nightmare sickness. He gives me *Ordeal of the Bodies*, a book he's written, the story of this child, this kid from the middle class. Sylvain is

135

lying naked on the black sofa, brown spots showing on his arms. 'Kaposi's,' he says, swallowing his AZT tablets. 'I've been HIV-positive for five years. By the arse, not the spike.' He falls silent and puts his thumb in his mouth. Sylvain always goes to sleep sucking his thumb, with his other hand resting on his teddy-bear's nose.

★ ★ ★

With Kader and Séverine from twelve-thirty till evening, till night. Scabs now cover the backs of my hands; the vein inside my elbow is shot. I've blown a good part of the dosh I set aside for new digs. Yesterday, sitting in a restaurant across from Jerome, I fainted into my plate, then did the same with the man with the dead arm, who said he couldn't guarantee that the kid-in-pain's mother would be published in September if I was still in this condition. My friends have disappeared. 'I can't stand it, you're a zombie.' 'We can't go on seeing you.' 'I'm telling you this for the good of your health. We'll stay in touch.' 'You've lost it intellectually. You don't listen anymore, and you don't hear a thing.' 'We can't stand the way you're making us look, and we don't have to.'

In the street and in the shops, people are walking around normally, without smack. How do they manage to be cool with nothing in their veins? In Sylvain's spare bedroom, I'm afraid of wetting my bed, wetting Sylvain's sheets. I've hit rock bottom. But I'm too much of a coward to take the final fix, the liberating overdose.

136

18 June, morning. In my suitcase I pack underwear, my toothbrush and razor, and two books. I shoot a half and climb into a taxi. The man with the dead arm has made an appointment for me at the Marmottan clinic.

In his dingy, cluttered surgery, the shrink seems asleep. I tell him I want to kick the habit, be hospitalized, I can't get clean by myself, I've already tried and always failed (silence). In a familiar tone, the shrink asks me how much I do, I say two to three grams a day (silence), he asks me my age, I say thirty-eight, that surprises him, he says with a smile that I'm old for an addict, I ask him if there's a right age to get hooked, he apologizes, says that wasn't what he meant, no there is no right age, but the addicts here are younger (a long silence, I feel he's bored stiff), he says I have to think it over, the treatment here is very hard no telephone no visitors no post and not much medicine, I tell him I don't get erections anymore and I'm wetting my bed (silence) he says that's normal I'll regain control over my bodily functions after I get clean (silence), he says I don't look in too bad shape so for starters I should try an outpatient treatment, he asks whether I want medicines, which ones, I dictate a prescription for

137

Mépronizine Seresta 50 Di-Antalvic, lots of Di-Antalvic it's better than Antalvic, Di-Antalvic contains paracetamol, he makes an appointment for four days hence to see how I'm doing. We didn't mention Jerome, he didn't ask. I wouldn't have said anything anyway; Jerome belongs to me, is in me, locked in my skull and my guts. It's eleven o'clock. I don't know where to go. I can't stay here; I have to leave before twelve-thirty, before I take a taxi to boulevard de Grenelle, before I go up to Séverine and Kader's clutching a one-cc insulin syringe from the corner chemist's.

At the Gare de l'Est, I swallow my medicine, wondering how many Gs a day you have to be shooting before they hospitalize you. Maybe it's a matter of appearances. I'm five foot ten; if I weighed eighty pounds, maybe I'd have a chance. I'm standing on the platform, waiting for a train to Thionville for two days with my old friends Françoise and Stéphane. They're too far away, always too far. I climb aboard the train, carrying eighty pounds too many and a dozen filters in my suitcase.

I didn't see much of Thionville; it was too ugly and depressing. Françoise and Stéphane met me at the station with Barbara, Alexandre and Frédéric, their radiant, blonde kids. That night, we ate at an outdoor café and washed the meal down with a few bottles of wine. Before going to sleep I took a double dose of medicine and shot my filters. I curled up in bed, thinking about the Marmottan shrink, about the half I've scheduled for the morning. All I have to do is hold out until tomorrow, until the first train back to Paris, until I get to Kader's, who will serve me a good half-wrap.

138

We went to the station buffet to wait for the train. Sitting in front of a cup of tea, I was shivering, sweat was running down my back, and through the fog generated by my Seresta – Di-Antalvic – filter-juice-hit-five-times I could hear Stéphane saying that I was going to die, that he didn't want me to die, that he loved me like a brother, I was his best friend, Françoise and the kids loved me too, we'd known each other for fifteen years. He put his hand on my trembling hand and stroked it. He asked me if I realized what I looked like, what kind of shape I was in. He said that it hurt him, that I was hurting him, and then he started to cry. I told him that I was going to kick the habit, that I was about to kick it, that I'd been thinking about it for months but now my mind was made up, that I was going to do it, in a few days. The train arrived, we hugged, Stéphane made me promise, and I did.

At the Gare de d'Est, I tell the taxi driver, 'Boulevard de Grenelle, please, and can you step on it? It's very urgent.'

In his red car, Kader dropped me off at Pelleport. It was close to midnight, Sylvain wasn't asleep yet. He read me the results of his latest tests: 310 T-cells, up from 236 last month. The doctor at Tarnier hospital says his condition is stable. Sylvain showed me a new dark spot on his right biceps. I went into my room and had a fix. 'It's the last one, Sylvain. Tomorrow, I'm kicking the habit.'

21 June, 8 a.m. I drink my tea, swallow my pills, go back to bed. Sylvain silently enters my room, sits down on a chair, his body bent, elbows on his knees, hands folded.

'How are you doing?'

'Bad. I'll never make it.'

I get up, hug Sylvain, and start crying on his shoulder.

I throw on my clothes and rush over to boulevard de Grenelle.

Jerome and I eat lunch at a restaurant in les Halles, and I accompany him back to the school. From his office, I phone the corpse-bearer and ask him to drive over right away, to take me to Marmottan. I kiss Jerome and he doesn't pull back; his mouth is almost alive. I steal a bit of his saliva and tell him it's better than all the medicine in the world. He says that isn't true, his eyes are elsewhere, he won't look at me.

The shrink still looks like he's asleep, the silences are still endless. I tell him that I can't do it, that the Seresta gives me anxiety attacks, that I want to be hospitalized. He doesn't answer, then he says he's going to prescribe something other than Seresta, which makes you climb the walls; something like Floxifrale, say.

23 June. One G, plus a half for tomorrow.

24 June. Drink tea, have a shit, shoot up, it's the last one, tomorrow I'm getting clean. It's a nice, early summer day, I'm walking through Paris, stopping at bars to drink beer. I'm not hungry, I'm thirsty. At Barbès that night, I'm hung over from the beers and the painful memory of my last fix. I fold a two-hundred-franc note and carry it in the palm of my hand. In rue Myrrha, an Arab asks me if I want something. I want a wrap of Paki, he leads me to a building entrance and extracts a wrap from between the laces of his trainers. I buy an insulin syringe and a lemon, order a cup

of coffee in a café in Goutte d'Or, take the teaspoon and lock myself in the lavatory. I'm preparing my last fix. Just as I dig the needle in, the café owner starts pounding on the door asking for her spoon, saying she'll call the filth if I don't clear off. I push the plunger. Tomorrow, Frank's getting married to his psychiatric nurse. I take a cab for Pelleport. Tomorrow.

IV

I swallow two Floxifrales and four Di-Antalvics with my tea, stretch out on the sofa, and wait for the pain. It comes quickly, but it isn't in my guts, it's spreading through my whole body, along the nerves, every nerve is excruciatingly painful and there's a freezing feeling inside my veins that's almost like burning. I phone the shrink to ask why my nerves and veins hurt so much, he answers that the pain isn't in either my nerves or my veins, but in my stomach. They're the 'cold-turkey cramps' you hear about, but the Di-Antalvic makes you feel the pain elsewhere. He asks if I've eaten, I tell him that I can't get anything down, and he gets angry. All you addicts are the same, he says, when you try to kick the habit you turn into vegetables, come on, you've got to eat, try some rice, you have to feed the cramps. I ask Sylvain to make rice for me, I don't have the strength. He makes me rice with chocolate, I eat a spoonful, but it makes me feel like throwing up. On the black sofa, I feel terribly cold inside. I look at the telephone a hundred times. I'll call Kader, just one fix, a little one, the last fix, no, it's too stupid, you have to hold out for three days, they're the worst, the most painful ones. I think of the days spent hurting, of the

145

zombies on rue Gaîté and elsewhere, a life wasted, spoiled, blown on powder. I close my eyes. Sylvain doesn't say anything, just walks quietly through the big, white, cold flat, and his silent presence soothes me. The evening of my first day of going cold turkey, I swallow two Mépronizines. A hellish night follows, full of dreams of powder and spikes. I'm turning to water, it's flooding through my skin and out of my arse. I don't have the strength to change the soaked sheets, I just push them down the bed with my feet, the mattress is soaked, too. I sit down on the toilet at three in the morning and pass water until seven. My arse and skin give off a disgusting smell and I feel an incredible burning in my lower back. I lay my head on one arm-rest of the sofa, my feet on the other, and the pain is bearable. I settle into my smell for that second, awful day. That night I piss in the sheets, Jerome rings up, his voice does me good. The shrink says it takes months to get back to normal, for the diarrhoea to stop, to regain your reflexes, your appetite, your zest for life. In the morning I wake up with my cock stiff. I try to make it come, stroking it up and down while thinking about Jerome, but it goes limp. That's to be expected, I tell myself. It'll be several weeks before it gets stiff during the day as well. Jerome, very strong. White juice, thick, living juice.

The third day is unbearable.

I slip into the bath for the first time in five days. I've arranged to meet Jerome at the place du Châtelet at twelve-thirty. This first day out of doors, my legs are wobbly, and the people, the cars and the streets all scare me. I'm afraid of the outside world, afraid of the time after we finish eating, of being without smack. In the

Chinese restaurant, he says I'm looking well. I'm cool,
I laugh, and I want him terribly as we go through the
imperial rolls, the fried shrimp, and the rosé de Provence. Jerome says he's leaving on holiday in three days,
talks about his fruit trees, his apple trees yielded far too
much last year, he didn't know what to do with so
many apples, the pear trees on the other hand, didn't
yield anything, but the strawberries were wonderful.
On the place du Châtelet, he says he'll ring me during
his holiday, and hopes I can hang on. We shake hands,
and when he says goodbye in his offhand way the
anxiety crashes down on me. I didn't have a lot to
drink, but it was too much after five days of going cold
turkey. I start thinking hard about smack. I walk up
boulevard Sébastopol, it's three o'clock, too early for
the métro dealers, so I take a bus to Port-Royal and
run into Ida in front of the Crystal.

'Hello, Ida, what's up? How's your job?'

'Done for. The bloke sold the shop.'

'What are you going to do?'

'I don't know. Hey, you've changed, you look
rested.'

'I got clean. It's been five days.'

'When I saw you, I thought so.'

'Anyone still dealing around here?'

'No, there's nothing happening. The owners of the
Crystal tipped the cops off that addicts were hanging
around their place.'

'You ought to kick the habit, Ida. I tell you, life
afterwards isn't the same, you're really cool.'

I'm lying. And I see my lie reflected in Ida's glance.

'Yes, I know. I'll have to get clean one of these days.
Well, I'm off. I have to meet Miniel; you know, the

147

Yugoslav. I'm dealing with him over by Saint-Michel. Ciao.'

'Ciao, Ida.'

She smiles with her rotten teeth and walks off, swinging her black bag. Ida's legs don't dance anymore; they look heavy, as if her beach sandals weighed a ton. Varicose veins crisscross her calves; her legs look a hundred years old. I sit down on a bench across from the Crystal as Ida disappears around the corner on to boulevard Saint-Michel. I run my finger along the scabs on my hand. Stroking my veins, I think of Jerome, and burst into tears.